Best wishes

Abigail ...

M000078951

Murder Under A
Bad Moon

A Mona Moon Mystery
Book Three

Abigail Keam

Worker Bee Press

ISBN 978 1 0824158 2 1
8 2 2019

Published in the USA by

Worker Bee Press
P.O. Box 485
Nicholasville, KY 40340

Madeline Mona Moon is not your typical young lady. She is a cartographer by trade, explorer by nature, and adventurer by heart.

She has inherited a fortune from her uncle and is one of the richest women during the Great Depression. But there's a problem. Miss Mona is accused of murdering her neighbor. Mona has made enemies in the Bluegrass, and the local sheriff has been ordered to make life difficult.

Why? Because Mona pays good wages to her employees and offers free health care. She even let her miners unionize. Mona is considered a radical and danger to some of the other horse owners. They want to be shed of Mona's *extreme* views.

It's too bad someone murdered Judge Landis Garrett, but if the evidence swings around Mona's way—all the better if it sticks many of the locals think.

Mona's response is to tell the sheriff and his cronies to go to hell. You want a fight? Well, bring it on!

That's how Mona does things in 1933.

1

Mona was in the fields checking on the foals with Kenesaw Mountain, her new farm manager, when Jamison drove up in a truck. "Miss Mona, you gotta come with me now."

"What's the problem?"

Not wanting to say in front of Kenesaw, Jamison repeated, "Come on, now."

Alarmed, Mona asked, "Has someone been hurt?"

"Not that kind of hurt," Jamison replied.

"Sorry, Kenesaw. I've got to go. Finish with the foals," Mona said, jumping into the truck. She didn't have time to complete her instructions as Jamison tore off, leaving ruts in the pristine field.

"Jamison, what is the matter?" Mona asked, holding onto the dashboard for dear life.

ABIGAIL KEAM

"Sheriff Monahan is at Moon Manor with a warrant for your arrest."

Astonished, Mona said, "That's crazy. Whatever for?"

"Sure 'nough crazy, but he's got his men looking for you. Miss Jetta has called Mr. Deatherage and told me to hide you good until he can get here."

"Where are we going?"

"My sister's house in Bracktown."

The truck found a bump in the road, and Mona's head hit the roof of the cab. Exasperated, she said "I still don't know what this is about. Why does Sheriff Monahan want to arrest me?"

"He says you done kilt Judge Garrett."

Mona gasped, "You mean Judge Garrett is dead?"

"Dead as dead can be. Sheriff Monahan says you done it.

Garrett was found by the Kentucky River. Miss Mona, that man was so mean, even dead, the waters of the river spat him out."

"Don't tell me. On the banks of Mooncrest Farm."

"Yes'am."

"Perhaps he fell into the river fishing, drowned, and was swept with the current."

"I don't think so, Miss."

"Why not?"

"Because Judge Garrett was missing his head."

"Oh, dear. Sounds ghastly."

"And that ain't all. His head was found in a bucket near one of our feed sheds. You is in trouble, Miss Mona, and so is everyone who works for y'all. They'll pin the blame on one of us working folk as your compatriot. Just wait and see. Sheriff Monahan is dirty as dirt."

Mona leaned back in her seat, taking in Jamison's information. She wasn't surprised Garrett was dead or that someone had murdered him. Judge Garrett was a nasty piece of work. His wife left him, his children disowned him, and his neighbors despised him. Even his dog loathed him.

It was the dog that had started Mona's battle with Judge Garrett.

That damn dog.

2

"Stop!"

Jamison stepped on the brakes and both were thrown forward. Catching his breath, he pulled over onto a grassy bank and looked curiously at Mona.

"I know you're trying to help but hiding makes me look guilty and a coward. Take me back, Jamison."

"Sheriff Monahan don't need evidence to take you in."

"So I've heard. I've run into trouble before. I can handle myself."

Jamison turned the truck around. "I hope so, but the South is different, Miss. People here don't cotton to Yankees, and they carry grudges for a long time. The Southern memory is long, and payback is violent."

Mona attempted to calm Jamison's fears. "Corruption is everywhere, even up North, but I have something up my sleeve. I have several friends who work on newspapers, and if I am unjustly arrested, they will write about it. I doubt Sheriff Monahan will want my arrest written about in the press."

"Yes'am. I sure hope you're right."

"I thank you for your concern, Jamison."

Jamison didn't reply, but drove up the long driveway to Moon Manor until he stopped before the front door.

Sheriff Monahan stood in the open doorway with a deputy arguing with Thomas, Mona's butler, who was blocking the entrance.

Mona stepped out of the truck. "Sheriff, how nice to see you."

"Your *boy* here was telling me that you was gone, Miss Moon," Sheriff Monahan accused.

Mona could hardly hide her revulsion. Before her stood a man who was the creature of the kingpin of Lexington—Billy Klair. Sheriff Monahan wouldn't be on her doorstep if Billy Klair hadn't have given the say so. He ran everything and everyone in Lexington.

Monahan reeked of sweat, his teeth were stained from tobacco juice, his face looked florid from drinking bootlegged whiskey, and his fat belly flowed over his belt. But he was clean shaven, his beige uniform crisp, and his badge shiny.

"One of my *men* fetched me. Please come in and have some lemonade. It's so warm for a fall day." Mona turned to her butler. "Thomas, please fetch us some refreshments."

She passed the two lawmen and beckoned them into Moon Manor, showing them into the library. "Please sit."

"I'd rather stand."

"Suit yourself, Sheriff. Isn't it customary for men to take off their hats inside, even in the South?"

Monahan stubbornly ignored Mona's request. "I'm here on official business, ma'am."

"It's miss, Sheriff. How may I help you?"

At that moment, Jetta Dressler rushed in with a pad and pencil, taking a seat by the window.

Chloe, Mona's standard-sized poodle, trotted behind Jetta, but upon seeing Mona rushed over wagging her tail in greeting. She sat next to Mona and leaned against her legs, looking up at her expectantly. Mona reached down and scratched her ears.

"What's she doing?" Sheriff Monahan asked, looking suspiciously at Jetta, who made squiggly lines on the pad.

"This is Miss Dressler, my secretary. I make it a policy that any official meeting with me must be recorded in case there is any confusion about who said what. Miss Dressler knows shorthand. She'll be transcribing everything we say. Is this an official meeting, Sheriff?"

"What do you know about Judge Garrett's death?"

Mona feigned surprise. "Landis Garrett is dead? This is terrible news. Sheriff, I insist you sit down and tell me what happened."

"I want to know what you had to do with it."

Mona pressed her hand against her heart. "Me? Why should I know anything about the man's death? Ah, here are our refreshments."

Thomas laid a tray of finger sandwiches and lemonade on a table and handed the sheriff and his deputy a tall glass. Seeing the guests were served, he stood by the door, not wanting to leave Mona with the two men.

Sheriff Monahan put his glass on the table. His deputy followed suit while Mona pretended not to notice.

Mona heard the front door open as Thomas went to greet whoever had just entered.

Dexter Deatherage strode into the library looking peevish but he hid it quickly, shaking the sheriff's hand. "Hello, Miss Mona. Sheriff Monahan. Miss Jetta. Deputy. Am I interrupting a social call?"

Mona said, "I don't know. Sheriff Monahan was just about to explain how Landis Garrett died."

"So Landis Garrett finally got his? Doesn't surprise me. Half the town hated him," Dexter said, standing close to Sheriff Monahan.

"That's not a nice thing to say about Judge Garrett," Sheriff Monahan said, narrowing his eyes at Deatherage.

Glaring back at the sheriff, Dexter replied, "Landis wasn't a nice man."

"You seem to assume Landis Garrett was murdered, Mr. Deatherage. How do you come by that opinion?"

"I wrangled with Landis yesterday in court about water rights on the west side of Mooncrest Farm. He was blocking a stream which was flooding onto Miss Mona's property during heavy rains. He looked fit as a fiddle, so unless he had a massive heart attack, I'd say someone did him in."

"As I understand it, the two of you came to blows."

Dexter chuckled. "Nothing so dramatic, Sheriff. A blow of words maybe. Everybody knows Landis resented Miss Mona and was causing her grief because she stopped him from beating his dog."

"You stole that dog, didn't you, Miss Mona?"

Mona said, "I took the dog to our vet. What happened to the dog after that, I don't know. I paid Landis for what the dog was worth and apologized. I hadn't realized Kentucky had no law keeping men from beating their dogs, or their horses, or their wives for that matter." Mona's implication hung in the air.

"Judge Garrett pressed charges of theft on you."

"I thought that very rude, especially after I had paid him for the dog. But the case was thrown out of court for lack of evidence, especially after I produced a bill of sale for the dog in Garrett's own handwriting."

"I hear it caused bad blood between the two of you."

"It certainly didn't cause us to have tea together on a regular basis."

"You tried to buy his farm."

"I did make an offer, but Garrett refused."

"And that made you mad."

"It certainly annoyed me, but I also made an offer to purchase Lord Farley's farm on the other side of me, and he's refused. Farley's still alive or so I've read in the newspapers. I don't have the habit of killing people who say no to me. I just find another way to get what I want."

"When was the last time you saw Judge Garrett?"

"I haven't laid eyes on Garrett since I stopped him from beating his dog with a riding crop. Mr. Deatherage has handled all contact with him since."

"On my counsel," Dexter added.

"How do you explain Judge Garrett was found dead on your property?"

"Was he?" Mona looked astounded. "Where?"

"He was thrown up on the sandbar near your boat dock."

"Thrown up? You mean he had been in the river?"

Sheriff Monahan nodded.

"Well, Sheriff. You must look for your culprit further upstream. He lives downstream from me. The Kentucky River doesn't flow backwards. Someone upstream must have killed him. And how do you know he was even murdered? Landis could have been fishing, fallen in, and drowned. Did you check to see if he had been drinking? Such accidents happen all the time."

"It would have been hard to tell, Miss Mona, since Judge Garrett had been decapitated."

Jetta looked up from her pad and gasped.

Sheriff Monahan threw a glance at her. "That's right for you to be shocked, Miss. Terrible business."

"Ghastly," Mona said.

"It looked like someone had taken an ax to him."

"This is terrible news. I didn't like the man, but I wouldn't wish anyone to go out that way," Mona said.

"So you admit you hated Judge Garrett?"

"I admit no such thing. I have a question for you. Hazel left Garrett six months ago after he broke her arm during a quarrel. Why didn't you arrest him for assaulting his wife?"

The deputy shot a quick look at the sheriff and shifted his feet. He was obviously embarrassed at Mona's insinuation of the sheriff's dereliction of duty.

"There was no evidence the judge was responsible for his wife's broken arm."

Dexter scoffed, "I would think Mrs. Garrett would know how her arm got broken, Sheriff."

"She was just an angry wife making senseless accusations."

"Like I said, Sheriff, Kentucky has no laws against beating one's wife," Mona said.

"I'm the one asking the questions here," Monahan said, trying to regain the upper hand against Mona and Dexter. "You said you haven't seen Judge Garrett the last couple of days, Miss Mona?"

MURDER UNDER A BAD MOON

"I told you I haven't seen Landis Garrett for months. Not after the dog incident."

"How do you explain his head being found in a bucket near one of your feed sheds?"

"I don't. I have no explanation other than someone planted his head there."

"Where were you, Dexter?"

"I have a complete record of my whereabouts for the past week. When was Landis murdered?"

"The coroner's report hasn't come in yet."

"Until the report is finished, I am going to call a halt to these questions."

"It's my job," Monahan protested.

Dexter asked, "Have you found the ax?"

"Not yet."

"So you don't even know an ax was used. You're just making wild accusations."

Sheriff Monahan turned to Mona. "I will need to talk to your men. Half of them were sent to jail by Judge Garrett."

"We wish to cooperate with you fully, but all my employees will have legal representation when you question them. You may investigate the area of my property where you found Judge Garrett and the feed shed, but for any other building or area of my property, you must have a warrant."

"I don't need no stinkin' warrant to do my job," Sheriff Monahan blustered.

Mona stood and smiled. "Ah, but you do. Everything must be done in the proper manner. The Mooncrest Enterprises Board of Directors will insist upon it. I'm afraid my hands are tied in this matter." She looked at her watch. "Oh, dear. I must cut this short. I have a speaking engagement with the League of Women Voters. Your wife is a member, is she not?"

Sheriff Monahan stood firm. He didn't like being dismissed by Mona Moon. He didn't like her at all. She was a Yankee, and besides, he didn't believe women should be in authority over men. It was against nature.

"Please excuse me, gentlemen. I must change. I certainly don't want to be late for the luncheon. They would demand an explanation," Mona said, making her warning clear.

Sheriff Monahan stood aside as Mona swept past him.

Jetta followed.

"Thomas, show Sheriff Monahan and his deputy out please," Dexter requested. He followed the two lawmen and the butler to the front door.

"I'll be in touch, Dexter," Monahan warned.

"Until then, give your wife my regards, Sheriff." Dexter and Thomas stood in the doorway until both men got into their car and drove down the road to the river. "Thomas, send someone after Kenesaw Mountain and tell him to come to Moon Manor. We need to have a powwow."

"Yes, sir."

"And Thomas."

"Yes?"

"Send word out to our men to be careful and stay as far away from the sheriff and his men as possible. Then I want to have a meeting with the house staff."

"Yes, sir."

Dexter turned and hurried up the stairs to talk with Mona and caution that she was treading on dangerous ground.

Thomas continued watching the car fade from his sight. "There goes one mean white man," he muttered before shutting the front door and locking it.

3

Violet answered the door and bade Dexter Deatherage into the master suite as Mona was gathering her hat and gloves after changing her dress.

"Mona, I need to talk with you before you leave for your meeting."

"Make it snappy. My car is waiting."

"I told you this would happen. You're making changes too fast. The folks around here think you're a Communist."

"I'm only instituting programs for my workers just as President Roosevelt is employing for the rest of the country. It's my patriotic duty, besides I hate to see misery when there is no need."

"Your programs are going to get you killed."

"Giving away free milk so my workers' children don't have rickets is going to get me killed? Balderdash."

Dexter soldiered on. "And letting your miners unionize. And paying your workers above the regular scale and giving them free medical care."

"The programs you describe cost Mooncrest Enterprises less than two percent of our total budget. Since the miners have unionized, we have not had one strike. You can't say that about our competitors. They are way behind us in copper production. And since I have instituted free milk and health care for our workers, our production overall has gone up—less work days missed and healthier workers. I don't call that Communism or socialism. I call that common sense and Christian to boot."

"So you admit to being a Christian. I've wondered."

"I admit I have no use for organized religion and its hypocrisy, just like I don't have use for so-called Christians and their hypocrisy. How many ministers in this town preach against the evils of drinking and then get kickbacks from the bootleggers selling to their flocks? What I've seen in this town is that religion is used to keep people down. I've seen it all over the world. It doesn't matter what religion, but when people brag about how good a Christian or a good Jew or a good Muslim or a good Hindu they are—look for a knife in your back."

"That's a little cynical for one so young," Dexter replied.

Violet spoke up. It hurt her sense of decency to hear Mona say such rash things. "Oh, Miss Mona, people are saying you are a heathen because you don't go to church. It would help folks' impression if you did. You do so much good for so many people. I hate to hear bad things said about you."

"Violet, dear, some people live their faith. Others go to church."

Violet twisted the handkerchief in her hands before responding, "I don't understand."

"I know, but you will one day. Give it time."

Dexter retorted, "Your social programs have brought the wolves to your door."

"Haven't you heard of *noblesse oblige*?" Mona countered.

"Haven't you heard of getting your head kicked in?"

"I think that is far from happening in the Bluegrass."

"Don't be too sure, Mona. You are disliked by a certain group of men. They're gonna try to take you down."

"Oh, Miss! Please listen to Mr. Deatherage," Violet groaned, grabbing Mona's arm.

Mona turned to her maid. "Don't worry, Violet. Nothing is going to happen to me. I've seen this before. These men don't like me because they can't control me. They don't like women giving orders, especially if it works to change the status quo. They want the workers in this town to be downtrodden and beaten. Well, not on my watch. My workers are going to be well treated. Mooncrest Enterprises is going to stand for something. Integrity for one thing. If these men want to treat folks like slaves and those folks stand for it, so be it, but not my people."

"They are complaining that your progressive policies are causing unrest amongst the other farm workers, and they're right," Dexter argued.

"Miss Mona, this town has a dark underbelly, and if people step out of line, there's always some knee bustin' or worse—lynching," Violet said softly. She knew of terrible things that had happened to people who had tried social change in Lexington, and she was afraid.

"The whole country is in an uproar because of this depression. It can't be just little old me causing all this anxiety. There are strikes, protests, and fights all over this nation. People are finally demanding reform and change—better pay, healthcare, and decent housing. I want to help President Roosevelt achieve these things."

Violet and Dexter exchanged glances. It was wonderful that their employer wanted to help the country realize these worthy goals, but did Mona understand that change came at a cost? The Old Guard wasn't going to give up their power easily.

Mona pulled on her gloves before glancing in the mirror and adjusting her hat. "Dexter, I hear what you're saying, but I've got to go. Hire whomever you need to hire to protect our interests."

"I think we need professional guards."

"Okay, get them."

"And I want to institute a policy that no less than three of our employees go into town any time, and that includes you, Mona."

"Jetta and Violet are coming with me to the League of Women Voters."

"Good, but I want to place a bodyguard with you."

"Now, Dexter."

"Don't *now Dexter* me. You've had guards before in the Near East."

"Please, Miss," Violet begged.

"See what you've done, Dexter. You've got Violet all shook up."

"Miss, listen to Mr. Deatherage. Some folks fix a notion in their heads and get themselves all riled up. Before you know it, someone ends up hurt."

"All right, Violet. Don't get into such a snit."

A knock sounded on the door, and Samuel poked his head in. "Sorry, Miss Mona. Mr. Deatherage. Kenesaw Mountain is in the library. You said you wanted to see him, sir?"

Dexter nodded and said, "Thank you, Samuel. Tell Mr. Mountain I'll be down in a moment."

"Walk me out," Mona said to Dexter.

"Of course."

She followed Samuel into the hallway and down the stairs to the front door where she turned and addressed the assistant butler. "Samuel, I'll be back between two and four. Please have tea ready for me. These luncheon meetings always have terrible food."

Samuel smiled in agreement and nodded, "Yes, Miss Mona. I know what you mean."

Violet followed while putting on her gloves, pausing only to lock Mona's bedroom door. She rushed to join the others.

Mona always insisted that all doors to her master suite be locked. Under the present circumstances, Violet thought it was prudent.

Dexter opened the Daimler's back door for Mona.

"Dexter, perhaps we should hire a private investigator to make inquiries? I don't trust Sheriff Monahan."

"Neither do I. He's more crooked than a dog's hind leg."

"I do trust your judgment, Dexter. Just protect the Moon family and the business."

"Tell my wife I'll be home late tonight, will you? Not to wait dinner for me. Wilhelmina will lord over the meeting today. She's bringing an old friend with her."

"Any friend of Willie's is a friend of mine. I'll make sure she gets the message. Ah, here's Miss Jetta. Right on time."

Jetta ran up to the car with a bag full of doo-dads she wanted Mona to hand out to the ladies at the meeting.

"What's in the bag, Jetta?" Mona asked.

"School pencils, erasers, and lollipops with the Mooncrest Enterprise logo on them."

"Very clever. Thank you for thinking of bringing them along. The ladies can give them to their children."

"Exactly," Jetta replied smugly.

Dexter helped Violet and Jetta into the car after Mona. Closing the car door, Dexter patted the side of the red and black Daimler giving Jamison the go-ahead to drive. He watched the car wind its way out of sight before heading back into the house to meet with Kenesaw Mountain. It was going to be a long day.

4

At the front door, Mona was greeted by the speaking committee, one of whom was her Aunt Melanie, who grabbed her aside.

She whispered, "We thought you might not come."

"Why not?" Mona asked.

"Because of the trouble at Moon Manor."

"You already know about that?"

"Sheriff Monahan's wife is here and was crowing about it until Mrs. Garrett showed up."

"You mean to tell me Hazel Garrett is here?"

"Yes, and that's not all. I don't think she knows."

Mona pulled off her gloves and put them in her purse. "Oh, dear."

"What do we do?"

"I think the president of the Women's Voters should handle this."

"That's Willie Deatherage."

"Is she clear-headed today?" Mona asked, smiling and searching for her friend who was also Dexter's wife and who had a penchant for drinking alcohol. She noticed ladies were watching her out of the corner of their eyes.

"Reasonably. I think Dexter sending her away to a sanitarium for a month has helped."

"I'm glad. I haven't seen Willie since she got back. I've been swamped with work."

Melanie hissed, "Shush. Here she comes now."

Wilhelmina Deatherage sidled up to Mona and Melanie. "Mona, my dear. So glad to see you. I can't wait to hear you talk about your adventures."

Mona leaned over and kissed Willie on the cheek. "My dearest. You are so pretty today."

"It's a wonder you remember what I look like."

"Now don't scold me, Willie. I know I've been amiss. I've been so busy, but I'll make it up to you. I promise."

"You can make it up by inviting my friend, Mary Breckinridge, and me for tea at Moon Manor today. She wants to see the renovations after the fire."

Mona turned her attention to the short, middle-aged, gray-haired lady standing quietly beside her friend. "Are you the Mary Breckinridge, who started the Frontier Nursing Service?"

"Yes, I am. I hope you don't hold that against me," Mary joked.

"Oh, my gosh. Miss Breckinridge, you should be giving the talk today—not me."

Mary laughed. "The ladies are sick of hearing me talk about what I do because I hit them up once a year for donations. They want to hear about your adventures, Miss Mona." She leaned in toward Mona in a conspiratorial manner. "Do you really keep a revolver in your purse?"

"Wouldn't you like to know?" Mona winked.

"Can we come for tea?" Willie asked.

"I would love to have you both for tea, but can I speak to you for just a moment, Willie?"

"Excuse us, please," Willie said to Mary and Melanie before she and Mona moved to a small antechamber. "What's up?"

"Landis Garrett is dead." Mona looked around to see if the ladies were watching them.

"I know. Dexter telephoned me after he got the word."

"He was found by the river, and his head was in a feed bucket on my property. I don't think today would be a good time to bring an illustrious person such as Mary Breckinridge to Moon Manor. The property is crawling with Sheriff Monahan's men."

"I think it is the perfect day to come to tea. Act as though nothing has happened, Mona. First rule of Southern society."

"What about Hazel Garrett?"

"She knows and will leave before your lecture starts to go to her apartment to await the notification of her husband's death."

"How did she find out?"

"I told her when she got here."

"How did she take it?"

"As I expected—sad and relieved, but not shocked. Landis was always the stink a skunk left behind."

"Tell me how you really feel, Willie."

"No one will mourn the passing of Landis

Garrett—not his wife, not his children, not most people in this town."

Mary Breckinridge joined Willie and Mona. "Excuse me, but Hazel Garrett wants to speak with you, Willie, before she slips out the back door."

"Excuse me," Willie said before she hurried to the kitchen where Hazel Garrett awaited her.

Standing alone with Mary Breckinridge, Mona felt awkward and a little star struck. "Miss Breckinridge, since you realize the situation I am currently in, you are most welcome at Moon Manor today, but I must warn you about associating with me at this critical time."

"It is because of your unique situation that Willie and I feel we must show our support, Miss Moon."

"Please call me Mona."

"Very well. Call me Mary. As I was saying, Willie has informed me of all the wonderful programs you have instituted for your workers. I am a firm believer in social reform, Mona. I believe in the Golden Rule. I would like to see for myself what you are doing, and I would like to visit Moon Manor again. I understand the housekeeper set the mansion on fire, but it has been restored."

"She's behind bars, thank goodness. You are familiar with Moon Manor, Mary?"

"I have a long history with Lexington. My grandfather, John C. Breckinridge, lived here and was Vice President under James Buchanan."

Mona's eyes widened. "And was Secretary of War for the Confederates."

Mary grinned. "The entire Breckinridge family has a rebellious streak. Look at me. As for Moon Manor, I knew your late uncle very well. I always hit Manfred up for a dollar or two as I hope to do to you as well."

"Tea will be right after this meeting. You and Willie can follow my car."

"Splendid. Ah, here comes our dear Willie. I think she wants to get started. I'll talk to you later."

Willie rang a bell. "Ladies. Ladies. Please take your seats. Lunch will be served in a few moments. We have a wonderful speaker today, and I am proud to name Mona Moon as one of my dearest friends."

"It helps that your husband is paid handsomely

by Mooncrest Enterprises," someone snidely quipped.

"It certainly does," Willie shot back, "or else I couldn't have afforded the new dress I'm wearing today. Besides being my friend and my husband's employer, Mona is a cartographer, explorer, and adventurer, following in the footsteps of Gertrude Bell. She is today's modern woman, taking her future into her own hands, and molding it as she sees fit. We are going to hear of her escapades in Iraq, and I hope she gives us the inside story of her latest adventure saving her friend, Lady Alice Morrell, which even made the headlines in the backwaters of Lexington. Ladies, I give you Miss Madeline Mona Moon."

Mona nervously stood before the large group of women who looked expectantly back at her. She knew they were the tastemakers of the Bluegrass, and their opinion of her would carry over into the community. Mona took a deep breath. It was do or die. She spoke haltingly at first, and then gaining confidence, began to regale the ladies with tales of wonder and the exotic.

Mona was going to make those women like her.

5

Violet ran into Moon Manor. "Thomas! Samuel! Come quick!"

Thomas, the butler of Moon Manor, ran into the hallway putting on his jacket. "Sorry, Miss Violet. Burl didn't call from the gatehouse telling us you had turned into the driveway."

"Is tea ready? There may be five joining Miss Mona."

"Didn't make sandwiches for that many ladies, but we'll tell Monsieur Bisaillon and he'll whip something up in a jiffy."

Violet smiled. She liked that Thomas was always so efficient. She could rely on him in any emergency. "Lovely."

Samuel asked, "Did it go well, Miss Violet?"

"Miss Mona was fabulous. She had the ladies

sitting at the edge of their seats, hanging on every word. You both would have been proud of her."

Thomas looked pleased until he heard talking in the driveway. "I think another car has pulled up. Samuel, inform the cook of more guests and set up the table in the parlor. I'll greet our guests and handle their hats and coats. Let's look smart."

Samuel rushed off to complete his tasks while Thomas opened the massive front door. He stood on the portico waiting to help if any lady needed assistance up the steps past the imposing lions into Moon Manor.

Mona stood with Jetta and Violet in a little knot waiting for Willie Deatherage and an older woman to exit a 1931 Cadillac.

Thomas recognized the older woman immediately—Mary Breckinridge! He wanted to run and tell the other staff, but maintained his post.

A yellow LaSalle raced up the driveway, screeched to a halt, and parked behind Willie. Aunt Melanie stepped out.

Mona waved everyone into the house.

Mary stood in the driveway, gazing at Moon Manor and remembering old times. She finally relented and followed the women. She stopped beside Thomas taking the ladies' jackets. "Hello, Thomas. I see you still guard the entrance to Moon Manor."

"Gosh, Miss Mary. It's so good to see you. Been a long time."

"We had many merry nights in this old relic of a house, didn't we?"

"Those days will never come again, ma'am."

"We were so young. Now look at me, Thomas. Gray hair."

"Me, too. Where did the years go?"

"I still can't believe Manfred is gone, and murdered, too. What a shock."

"Miss Mona put his passing to right."

"Is she a good employer, Thomas?"

"She takes care of her own. That's what's bringing trouble her way."

"I believe in what Mona's trying to do. Coming to tea is making a public statement that I am in agreement with her. I ran into the same issues when I began the Frontier Nursing Service. I never understood why people were against me helping women and children with health care."

"Some people have a meanness in their bones."

"Is Sheriff Monahan still on the property?"

"I think he's gone into town to get a search warrant for the house."

"When he comes back, you better watch him like a hawk. He's known to plant evidence, or so I've heard."

"Yes'am."

"I'd better go in. Mona will wonder where I've gone off to."

Thomas let Mary pass and then shut the door, locking it soundly. He didn't want the sheriff to barge in when the ladies were having their tea.

He followed Mary into the parlor where Samuel was already serving the ladies. He perused the tea service and was pleased with its arrangement. Samuel would make a fine butler one day, and hopefully would take Thomas' place when he retired. Thomas was feeling a deep aching in his bones and dreaded Kentucky winters. Like Mary Breckinridge, he was getting old.

6

Enjoying her tea, Mary said, "Wasn't lunch terrible?"

Willie twittered and added, "I wasn't going to say anything but the mashed potatoes were lumpy and the chicken was overcooked. Talk about dry. I'm going to have to find somewhere new for our luncheons."

Mary put down her teacup and looked about the parlor. "Mona, you've done a wonderful job restoring Moon Manor. I'm glad you decided to paint the public rooms white. It was so gloomy before with all the dark paneling. Looks up-to-date now."

Melanie sniffed at Mary's comment.

Mary said, "Not that Moon Manor wasn't impressive before, but it was so Victorian. Sorry,

35

Melanie. Did I offend you?"

"You knew my father, Mary?" Mona asked, not allowing Melanie to complain about the renovations at Moon Manor. Melanie was constantly harping about Mona's alterations—among other things.

Mary replied, "Just to say hello. He was several years older than I, but he was a very striking looking man. I also remember your mother. She was lovely."

Mona laughed. "Thank you, but people are always saying I look like Jean Harlow." Mona turned to Willie. "I did finally see a Jean Harlow picture with Clark Gable. Oh my, it was racy. It looked like Harlow wasn't wearing any undergarments."

Selecting several egg salad sandwiches with the crust cut off, Mary said, "You do have the Moon coloring, Mona. I would have recognized you for a Moon anywhere—the white hair, alabaster skin, and unusual eyes. Amber aren't they?"

Mona nodded.

"You know your Uncle Manfred was closer to my age, and I knew him best of all the Moons. I was very sorry to hear of his passing, especially under such horrible circumstances. It was quite shocking, really," Mary said.

Melanie finally got a remark in. "One can never tell about the murderous intents of servants. Look what happened to Mamah Cheney and Frank Lloyd Wright at Taliesin. That servant killed seven people with an ax while burning the house down around their heads."

Jetta shot a conspiratorial look at Violet, who bowed her head to hide her embarrassment and anger at Melanie's remark.

"That was close to twenty years ago. Can't we talk about something more cheerful other than murder?" Willie complained. "What did you think of Mona's employee programs she outlined in her talk today?"

Mary thought for a moment and chose her words carefully. "One of the reasons you are meeting resistance is due to deeply held beliefs in a rural community. After all, Lexington alone has 1704 farms. Despite being the home of Transylvania University and University of Kentucky, Lexington is rather . . . how should I say this . . . conservative in its thinking. People believe charity and relief should come from churches and private organizations. They're having trouble wrapping their minds around the idea that government regulations can make things better, but they are so desperate, they are willing to try. At least, some are. The Old Guard is resisting. They are used to running things. You can't imagine the opposition I met when I started the Frontier Nursing Service."

Mary puffed up her chest and imitated men speaking. "'Why should a well-bred lady like yourself want to ride horseback into those hollers, helping those hillbillies?' 'Little lady, you should be at home, cooking dinner for your husband.' 'Mary Breckinridge, your grandfather would roll in his grave if he knew you spent your time among those ignorant bootleggers in the Appalachian Mountains.'"

The other ladies chuckled at Mary's impersonations. They recognized two of the men she was mimicking.

"But I'm not using taxpayers money to address social and health problems with Moon Enterprises employees. It's Moon money. Why do others give a damn?" Mona asked.

"Because you make them look bad, and they might have to dig into their pockets as well if too much heat is put on them," Mary said.

"I don't think churches and charity organizations can address the country's problems we're having. This is a world-wide crisis, and help must come from the top down. Not from the bottom up," Willie added.

Mary said, "I agree, and so do others, which is why voters switched from President Hoover's economic policies to Roosevelt's New Deal."

Mona set her teacup on a side table. "I'm only practicing his new guidelines for employment—shorter working hours and better pay."

"Which is why you must carry on, dear. Others in this community will look to you for guidance. If you reap good results following President Roosevelt's guidelines from the National Recovery Act, the others will follow suit."

"We already have good results. Because I have a doctor come once a month, the number of employees missing work is considerably down. All workers have a tetanus shot, and children have the diphtheria vaccine. We have taught the women methods to fight lice other than combing turpentine through their hair. Miss Jetta is helping our workers earn their high school diplomas. She found that many don't know how to read and write very well. She has five students currently enrolled in the program she has set up."

Jetta explained, "It's slow going. We had seven students but two dropped out. They said it was too hard, but the other five seem committed. I hope that all of Moon employees have a high school diploma eventually, or at least, have to opportunity to earn one."

"Even Violet is pitching in by teaching sewing," Mona added.

Violet blushed. "I just started. Miss Mona lets me use the ballroom where we have set up tables. Last week, I showed how to select the correct fabric for an outfit and how to cut a pattern. I have two students, but I hope to have more."

"Two are a beginning. More will come," Mona commented, smiling at Violet.

"Why can't their mothers teach them?" Melanie asked.

"Because they're too busy cooking, cleaning, and taking care of their babies," Willie said, rolling her eyes.

"I guess we'll see a lot more of those dreadful feed sack dresses then," Melanie grumbled.

There was a painful silence as Melanie chewed on a cookie, not noticing Violet was wearing such a dress.

"Melanie, I swear. I could just slap the asinine out of you," Willie snarled.

Melanie looked astonished. "What? What did I say?"

"You hold classes in the ballroom?" Mary asked, ignoring Melanie. She always thought Melanie to be a vapid individual.

"It's a huge room and just sitting there not being used, so why not?" Mona said.

"As a nurse and reformer myself, I must commend you on your fight to improve things. You must be very proud that Mooncrest Farm is leading with innovative programs during this national crisis, Melanie." Mary couldn't give up the temptation to goad Melanie.

Melanie looked dubious. "I think our programs are why a dead man was found on Mooncrest property. As you said, Mary, the Old Guard will not give up their power easily. They are going to try to pin this murder on Mona or someone from here on the farm."

"That's why I felt it so important to come to tea. I still have connections in the political world and am held somewhat in national prominence. The Breckinridge name still means something. I thought it important I show support."

Willie interjected, "Yes, your visit will be all over town tomorrow, and I hope in the paper. I—we can't thank you enough."

"Didn't you know Landis Garrett, Mary?" Melanie asked, while motioning to Thomas for more tea.

"I met him when I came to visit my relatives. We ran in the same crowd before I went back to Europe." Mary was thoughtful for a moment. "Even then, he showed signs of being difficult. He was sweet on me, but I made sure he understood I was attracted to another. He soon lost interest, and took up with poor Hazel. I hear her life has been a bag full of copperheads."

Mona asked, "Landis was difficult in what way?"

"To put it plainly, he was mean. He had a grubby soul."

"A grubby soul?" Mona blurted out.

Willie stated, "Mary, you think he was born bad?"

"Some people are bad because of circumstance. Landis was awful because he enjoyed the chaos. He was always causing mischief. It's not surprising he was murdered. And you saw how Hazel took his death. She hardly blinked at the news."

Melanie piped up. "Perhaps she killed Landis."

Willie scoffed, "And then cut his head off and threw him in the river? I hardly think so. The woman is so frail, she can barely pick up a newspaper."

"She had help," Melanie said, wrinkling her nose. "I know I would have killed Landis long before this."

"The fact that he was found on Moon property is a message. I think every Moon employee needs to be alert and cautious," Mary warned.

"Which doesn't include me, I hope," Melanie said. "I've never agreed with Mona's policies."

"Which you've made abundantly clear publicly," Mona said bitterly.

Mary accepted a lemon tea cake from Thomas. "Melanie, I've known you since you were born. I've held you on my knee in this very house. Those who seek to destroy the house of Moon will try to divide it first. Don't make the same mistake the South did in the Civil War. Even if you don't agree with Mona, show a united front. The two of you are stronger together than apart."

Melanie was taken aback by Mary's warning and nervously took a sip of her tea, almost spilling it.

"Is there anything else you can tell us?" Willie asked.

"If Billy Klair isn't behind the death of Landis Garrett, he knows who is. Be careful with him," Mary said.

"I don't know why you all are always ganging up on Billy. He's done a lot for this town," Melanie said.

"Yeah," Willie sniped. "Like putting his hand in everyone's pockets."

Melanie made a sour face at Willie. "He was the very heart of changing the law where women could have the same rights to their children as men in a divorce or separation. Before that law, the courts always awarded guardianship of the children to the fathers. Can you imagine any of my husbands having control over my children?"

"Mary, why did you become a nurse? You could have led a life of ease," Mona asked, wanting to change the subject from Billy Klair, the kingpin of Kentucky.

"There were many reasons. I was tired of being a rich woman who was idle, but the main reasons were very personal. My marriage to my second husband was not good. He ran around on me, so I divorced him. It was easy to do after my two young children died."

"I'm sorry," Mona said, embarrassed she had asked such a tactless question.

"Don't be. After my divorce, I sat around in my big house mourning until I decided to quit feeling sorry for myself. I could go on being useless, or I could actually do something to help people. When I lived in Europe, I had the good fortune to see midwives in action and was impressed with the health care they provided to mothers and children. I got my nursing degree, came back to Kentucky, bought some horses to ride into the backwoods, and started the Frontier Nursing Service. The rest, as they say, is history. Besides myself, there are now ten women, who ride into the most remote parts of the mountains to offer health care."

Jetta said, "You and your work are most inspirational, especially to working women like myself."

Mary reached over and patted Jetta's hand. "Thank you, my dear. Your words mean so much to me. And with that, I must take my leave. Willie, I need you to drop me off at the Phoenix Hotel. I leave early in the morning for Hyden, Kentucky. The pregnant ladies of the mountains await."

Mona stood. "I can't tell you what an honor it is to meet you, Mary."

"Keep up the fight, Mona Moon. We need women like you if the world is to change." Mary turned to Melanie and lied one of those little white lies society needs to keep spinning in a positive light. "Melanie, my dear. It was wonderful to see you again."

"Just a minute," Willie said. "Hold on to your britches, Mary. You need money, don't you?"

"Always."

"Mona, why don't you hold a fundraising ball for the Frontier Nursing Service and other organizations in town?"

Mona spat out, "Not another ball, Willie. I've barely recovered from the last one."

Not deterred, Willie said, "Halloween is coming up. It can be a masquerade ball."

"You're not endearing yourself to me, Willie," Mona said, amused at Willie's enthusiasm.

"We can make it the social event of the year."

"I thought my Derby party in May was the social event of the year," Mona remarked.

Ignoring Mona's quip, Aunt Melanie asked, "How Willie? Everyone puts on a party starting Labor Day all the way through New Year's Eve."

Willie said, "You're right, Melanie. We need to stand out. What we need is an attraction everyone will want to see."

"Get a movie star," Thomas said quietly.

Willie blurted out, "You're a genius, Thomas."

"How are we going to get a movie star?" Mona asked.

"Leave it to me. First of all, have all your nurses attend, Mary. Every bachelor in town will come if he knows single girls will be at the party."

"Oh, Willie, you're the cat's meow," Mona laughed.

"I know. You can ask the Bambino," Thomas suggested.

"Who?" Willie asked.

"The Bambino. The Sultan of Swat. Babe Ruth," Thomas said. "People will come from all over to see Babe Ruth."

Everyone turned and looked at him.

Mona echoed, "Babe Ruth?"

"Why not? He does a lot of charity work, and if you pay his expenses, I'm sure he'll come, especially if you tell him you have a full wine and bourbon cellar. The man likes to drink," Thomas explained.

"And whore around," Melanie sniped.

Willie shot back, "What man doesn't."

Melanie raised an eyebrow. "That's a mouthful, Willie. Having trouble at home?"

Mona inquired, "Doesn't Ruth have to play in the World Series?"

"The Yankees won last year. It's not sure they'll play this year, but the World Series will be over by then, Miss Mona," Jetta said.

Mona asked, "What do you think, Thomas?"

Melanie almost choked on her lemon tart. It was bad enough that Mona's maid and secretary were allowed to join them at tea, but now the butler was butting in on the conversation and Mona was asking him what he thought. Her mother would roll over in her grave if she knew Mona was treating the servants like equals. Personally, Melanie couldn't stomach it. Mona held the family purse strings, and Melanie had signed an agreement not to criticize Mona or Mooncrest Enterprises publicly or she would lose her stipend. So she looked attentive and hid her resentment of allowing Thomas to voice a suggestion. This was the way the world was now, and she had to adapt, but it was a bitter pill to swallow.

Thomas chose his words carefully. "If Babe Ruth came to Moon Manor, folks would pay for the privilege of coming to your party, Miss Mona. You can have an outdoor shindig where average folks pay twenty-five cents to hear Mr. Ruth give a small talk and hit a few balls and then charge the rich folks twenty-five dollars a couple to attend a party in the ballroom later that night."

Willie suggested, "I think children should be allowed in for free."

"Twenty-five dollars! That's a lot of money," Mona said.

Jetta gushed, "We can buy Baby Ruth candy at a nickel and sell the bars for a dime."

Mary looked at her wrist watch. "Wilhelmina, I've really got to go. I'm sure you ladies will work out the details later."

"Of course. Let's get you back to the hotel, Mary. I know you have a long day ahead of you tomorrow. Well, ta ta ladies. Jetta, you and Thomas put your heads together and come up with more ideas. I'm so excited about this," Willie said.

Samuel met the women at the door with their coats as Willie swept out the front door with Mary Breckinridge.

Mona followed them out with Violet and Jetta tagging behind. They waved until they couldn't see the car anymore.

Melanie hurried down the steps without saying goodbye and jumped into her car. She honked her horn as her yellow LaSalle sped down the driveway.

Mona turned to Jetta and Thomas. "I haven't agreed to anything yet. Hand me a written proposal, and I'll make my decision after going over it."

Energized and full of excitement, Jetta said, "I'm going to work on it now. Thomas, let me know if you have any more ideas on how to work this."

"Yes, Miss Jetta."

Mona stared at Violet who was listening.

"Don't you have anything to do?"

"Yes, Miss Mona. I have mending."

"Then hop to it."

"Yes'am." Violet ran to get her sewing basket.

Thomas shut the front door.

"Thomas, I want a few words with you."

Thomas followed Mona into the parlor.

"Did I speak out of turn, Miss Mona?"

"Did it bother you that I entertained Mary Breckinridge, the granddaughter of John Breckinridge? He was so prominent in the Civil War and adamant about keeping slavery a state's right."

"Did it bother you that you had politicians at your Derby party who voted against the right for women to vote in this country?"

51

"Quite frankly, it did. You and I have a similar problem, Thomas. There's always someone trying to stop us from being free. I, because I'm a woman, and you because of the color of your skin."

"I say let the past stay in the past. Miss Mary is not her grandfather, and she's trying to do right in the world. So are you, but sometimes we don't have the luxury to act and speak as we feel."

"I think you are telling me to keep my feelings under wrap as there are other things to consider. I respect that, Thomas."

"Thank you, Miss Mona. Is that all?"

"Yes. You may go."

Thomas started to leave but stopped and turned. "Miss Mona, did you know one of my ancestors fought for the Confederacy and won a medal for bravery?"

"A white ancestor?"

"No, he was black. Don't that beat all?" Thomas replied without a hint of irony.

Mona nodded. She caught Thomas' meaning. Life was strange, and when you thought you figured it out, something odd jumped up and bit you on the fanny.

7

Mona was working in her office when Dexter stormed in. She looked up from her notes and said, "Yes?"

"Sheriff Monahan is here with a warrant to search Moon Manor."

"Just as he promised. Is everything in place?"

"The Pinkerton guards are set up, and I have junior members of my law office who will follow the sheriff and his men around as witnesses. Every room has been photographed today with a time stamped on the picture, and we will have photographers who will snap everything again that Sheriff Monahan's man photographs. That's the best we can do."

"Can he still plant evidence?"

"Yes, but it will be harder to do with all of our

people here and the photographs. We'll use the evening paper to validate the date and time frame in the photographs."

"He will probably order everyone from the house."

"Legally, Monahan can't do that. A person has the right to monitor a search, but yes, he will bluff such an order which is why I went to Judge Angelucci for a court order allowing our people to stay during the search." Dexter gave Mona a wicked grin. "Just in case."

Mona grinned back. "I like the way you think, Counselor." She stood and smoothed her dress. "Let the sheriff in." She followed Dexter into the foyer and nodded at Thomas to unlock the front door.

Thomas unlocked the door and opened it wide to let in the lawmen.

Mona strode forward and accepted the search warrant Sheriff Monahan handed to her.

Violet and Jetta stood on the landing overlooking the foyer. Jetta stood calmly, although Violet trembled slightly.

"Miss Madeline Mona Moon, I am here to search Moon Manor for any evidence pertaining to the death of one Landis Garrett."

"Everyone at Moon Manor will be happy to cooperate, Sheriff. We want to bring justice to the person or persons who murdered the judge as much as you do. Search away."

The sheriff motioned his men to separate into three groups which splintered into the parlor, library, and upstairs. Following one group into the parlor, he came storming out into the foyer where Mona and Dexter were waiting. "What's the deal with the Pinkerton man and one of your boys taking pictures of us making our sweep? That's against the law."

Dexter handed Monahan a court order attached to a blue sheath of paper. "We have authority to photograph and witness the search."

"That ain't right."

Dexter replied, "I assure you, it is legal. A Fayette County judge says it's so. See his nice big John Hancock at the bottom of the page. You can search anywhere in Moon Manor, but with witnesses who may take notes and photographs. We also have the right to list and photograph anything you take off the premises. This is as much for your protection as it is for ours."

"What does that crack mean? Are you accusing me of foul play?"

"I'm not accusing anyone of anything. Mona Moon and Mooncrest Enterprises are cooperating to the fullest extent of the law."

"You're interfering with an investigation is what you're doing," Sheriff Monahan groused, trying to intimidate Dexter by bellying up to him.

Mona tapped him on the shoulder and whispered, "Sheriff, your men need you, and I need for this search to be over soon. The Lt. Governor and his wife are coming soon. My staff needs to set the dining table, and I need to get dressed."

"Happy Chandler is coming here?"

Mona nodded. "And soon."

A deputy came up and beckoned Monahan aside.

"What did you find in the office?" Mona overheard the sheriff ask.

"Nothing. There are no files, account books, or correspondence of any importance. Just some fruit cocktail and angel food cake recipes."

"Fruit cocktail recipes!"

Monahan strode over to Mona and Dexter. "Where are your files on Garrett?"

Mona looked innocent. "I have no file on Landis Garrett."

"No correspondence concerning him taking you to court about the dog or the lawsuit you filed against him over the water flooding your land?"

Mona folded her hands calmly in front of her dress. "All that information would be at my attorney's office and is confidential. No judge will ever grant you a warrant to search an attorney's office."

"We'll see about that," Monahan huffed, sweat breaking out on his brow. He pulled out a handkerchief and patted the back of his neck. That small gesture gave him time to reflect. He did not want a tongue lashing from Albert "Happy" Chandler, who had presidential aspirations. The Lt. Governor's appearance at Moon Manor was sending a message loud and clear. Making a decision, he called out, "Let's wind it up, boys."

Within ten minutes, his men were filing out the door. As Monahan took his leave, he warned Mona, "I'll be watching you, missy. Don't even spit on the sidewalk because I'll be there."

"Why would I ever spit on a sidewalk, Sheriff? That type of filthy behavior spreads TB." Putting a smile on her face, Mona escorted Monahan to the portico. "Thanks for stopping by. I hope you catch the killer soon." She beckoned to four Pinkerton guards holding shotguns. "These men will escort you safely off Moon property."

Monahan was angry, but tipped his Stetson hat politely and waved his index finger in the air, giving the signal for his men to load up the vehicles.

The Pinkertons also got into a car and followed until the sheriff and his men exited from Moon property.

When the cars were out of sight, Dexter asked, "Are the Chandlers really coming to dinner?"

"They are stopping by for a drink before they go to Aunt Melanie's house for dinner. Mildred wants a private tour of the renovations."

"Mentioning Chandler's name stopped Monahan cold today, but he won't quit. He'll keep on plugging until he finds something. It's personal for him now."

"Let's worry about him tomorrow." Mona

took Dexter's arm as he escorted her back into the house. "Why don't you stay to have a drink with the Chandlers?"

"I have things to attend to but thanks for the offer."

"Of course, but you must excuse me. I've got to change this dress before my guests arrive."

"Surely. I'll be at the office tomorrow. Call if you need anything."

Mona ran up the stairs where Violet waited for her on the landing. It had been a trying day for both women, and the strain showed on Mona's face. A nice hot bath would calm her nerves, but it would have to wait.

Violet would have to help her get ready or she would be late for her own cocktail hour!

8

Mona wore a silver chiffon cocktail dress with white flying cranes on the bottom left side with a plain chiffon mantle wrapped around her shoulders. Hearing voices float up the staircase, she hurried downstairs to find Lt. Governor Albert "Happy" Chandler and Mildred Chandler being entertained by Jetta. "Albert and Mildred. How nice of you to stop by for a drink before you go to Melanie's house."

"Now, Miss Mona, I've told you before to call me Happy."

"Forgive me." Mona turned to Mildred. "Can I get you something?"

Mildred pushed a large pheasant feather threatening to escape her new hat out of her face. "Jetta got me a gin and tonic. I'm fine. These canapés are wonderful. Dates stuffed with cream cheese and walnuts. Goes with your talk about the Near East, doesn't it? I just clipped a recipe from the Ladies Home Journal for peanut butter and pickle canapés."

Happy said, "I can't wait until Prohibition is repealed. I've run out of bourbon at home, and we have to bother our neighbors if we want to enjoy an adult beverage."

Mona laughed. "I hope my liquor cabinet isn't the only reason you come to see me."

Happy teased, "No. It's your liquor *cellar,* which causes me to visit."

"I understand beer can be sold legally now," Mildred commented. "The problem is I've never had a taste for beer."

"Nothing like a cold beer and a hot dog with all the trimmings at a baseball game during the summer," Happy said.

Accepting a sherry from Jetta, Mona said, "I understand you have a great interest in baseball, sir."

"I love all sports, but mighty partial to America's favorite pastime. As a young man, I considered a career in professional baseball, but finally decided on the law."

"Speaking of the law, I hear Landis Garrett is dead. Murdered!" Mildred said, lowering her voice.

"Yes," Mona responded. "And he had the bad manners to wash up on my property."

Mildred leaned forward and whispered, "Is it true about his head?"

Mona answered, "That's what Sheriff Monahan tells me. I haven't been to where the body was discovered."

"I'm sure Dexter Deatherage has everything under control. I see you have hired Pinkertons though. Why is that?" Happy asked.

"We've been getting threats. I need to keep my employees safe until the murderer is apprehended."

Happy started to ask more questions, but Mildred interrupted him. "I also hear your talk at the League of Women Voters was stupendous. I wish I could have been there."

"I hope the women enjoyed my talk. All I can say is that I did my best to be entertaining and informative."

Happy groused, "Enough of this syrupy chatter about Miss Mona's lecture. I want to know about Landis Garrett's murder. I know Melanie will have loads to say about it, but I want to hear it from the horse's mouth."

Mildred looked sheepish. "Melanie does have a tendency to embellish facts."

"All I can say is I got word that Judge Garrett's body was discovered by my property line at the Kentucky River, and his head turned up in a feed bucket near one of my storage sheds. Sheriff Monahan searched Moon Manor this afternoon. That's all I know."

Happy whistled. "Decapitated. What a way to go."

"It doesn't surprise me," Mildred said. "It was probably some irate husband who did him in."

"What makes you say so?" Mona asked, putting a date on her plate.

"Oh, Landis played around on Hazel. He was a notorious ladies' man."

Happy chimed in, "There's an old story he propositioned a serving wench at his own wedding."

"Do you believe the story?" Mona asked.

"It has a ring of truth to it. He favored women from the lower classes of our society," Happy said.

Mona said bitterly, "Women who could least afford to offend Landis by turning him down."

"I couldn't stand him myself," Mildred confided. "He once pinched me at a garden party, and when I confronted him about it, he told me I should be pleased at his attention. Of all the impudence. I wanted to throw my fruit punch in his face, but I didn't. I just made sure I was never within his reach again."

"Perhaps if more women had thrown things at Landis, he might have kept his hands to himself," Mona suggested.

"One doesn't like to cause a scene," Mildred said.

Mona grinned. "I think women should get over that."

Happy said, "This stays on the down low, but my bet is that Hazel got fed up with Landis' philandering."

Mildred shook her head. "Hazel is not strong enough to cut off someone's head. How was the old goat's head cut off anyway?"

"The sheriff thinks it was with an ax. They've

been looking for it on Mooncrest property. Why, I don't know. I think Landis was killed upstream and tossed into the river."

"That doesn't explain how his head wound up in a bucket," Happy said. "Someone deliberately put that head on your property to make a point."

"I understand he was a hard judge," Mona said.

Mildred sniffed. "I heard he got a young girl from Irishtown in the family way. That's the real reason Hazel left him."

"There's a motive right there. Who is the girl?"

Mildred answered, "Can't say. It's been hush hush."

Mona asked, "If it's so hush hush, how do you know about it, Mildred?"

"I have my sources."

"Give. What's the girl's name?"

"All I know is her first name might be Clare."

Happy looked at his wife in amazement. "You are a fountain of misbegotten information. Next time I need mud on an opponent I must come to you."

Mildred smiled and then said, "That's all I

know. Really."

Mona said, "If you hear anything else, let me know. I think Sheriff Monahan is gunning for me."

"Keep him away from Melanie then. She likes to offer backhanded compliments. It's her specialty. I should know because she's done it to me several times," Mildred confided.

"Land o' Goshen, why are we going to her house for dinner then?" Happy complained.

"Because Melanie's a big contributor to your campaign, darling."

"Oh, yeah. That's right. And speaking of dinner, let's go, dear."

She put down her drink and stood. "Thank you, Mona. It was lovely to chat and have a drink with you. Don't let the sheriff get you down, but don't underestimate him either. He's a cunning man."

"Thank you for the warning, Mildred," Mona said, walking the couple out.

Happy turned to Mona. "I think it might be a good idea to keep those Pinkertons for a while. At least, until things simmer down."

"What have you heard, Happy?"

Chandler put on his hat. "I hear things, too, but can't tell you from whom or why. Just keep those good old boys handy." He winked at Mona before joining his wife in their car.

It was obvious the Chandlers were warning Mona of a grave danger since they had invited themselves for cocktails. She wished they had been more forthcoming, but she would start with the clue of a young girl named Clare in Irishtown.

After all, how many unmarried pregnant girls named Clare could there be in the Irishtown?

9

Mona walked into a small neighborhood grocery store and browsed the meager shelves until the store's two customers left. Approaching the clerk, she asked, "Excuse me. I was wondering if you could help me. I'm looking for a young woman by the name of Clare in this neighborhood. Can you direct me?"

The middle-aged clerk peered over his round, horn rimmed glasses at Mona. "Lots of Clares around here. Can you be more specific?"

"She is unmarried and young."

"Are you one of them do-gooders from a church or something?"

"I might be. My mission is delicate if you know what I mean." Mona did not want to come right out and ask for a young unmarried pregnant

68

woman. Clare might not yet be showing.

The clerk shrugged and busied himself with stocking shelves behind the counter.

Feeling a wisp of hair escape, Mona quickly tucked it back under her hat covering her platinum mane. She certainly didn't want anyone to identify her by her unique hair color. Catching the clerk's attention, Mona took a five dollar bill from her purse and laid it on the counter. "Do you remember now?"

The clerk reached for the five dollars but Mona slammed her hand over it. "Clare?"

"White house with green shutters on Pine Street." The clerk tried to slide the money from Mona's hand, but she pressed it against the nicked wooden counter.

"Lots of houses have green shutters."

"Yeah, but this one is missing most of them."

Mona removed her hand from the bill. "Thank you. You've been most helpful."

The clerk grabbed the bill and studied it. "This is more than I take in the store for a day sometimes."

Mona didn't reply as she was walking out the door to her car. "Jamison, do you know where

Pine Street is?"

"Yes, Miss Mona."

"Park a block from it. I'll get out and walk."

"Irishtown is no place for you to be walking by yourself. It's a rough part of town."

"I'll be fine. Besides, I have my *little friend* in my purse."

Jamison did as bidden and parked under a shade tree two blocks over from Pine Street.

Mona got out and walked in the street as there were no sidewalks and traffic was sparse. The day was warm, so women sat on their porches snapping green beans. Some waved at Mona in greeting, wondering who she was. Occasionally, Mona heard a baby cry or a couple arguing as she passed the weather-beaten shotgun houses.

Several men lollygagged near a dilapidated car with the hood up. One of them hissed something nasty at Mona as she walked by.

"Excuse me. Were you addressing me?" Mona asked the man.

"You heard me," the man said, slurring his words slightly.

Mona took inventory of the man quickly. He was unshaven, hollowed-eyed, and looked beaten down by the Depression, but that didn't mean she was going to put up with being a whipping boy for his anger. "No, I really didn't. Can you please repeat yourself so others may hear as well?"

Stunned that Mona wasn't embarrassed or afraid, the man scowled and stole away.

The other men refused to meet Mona's eyes and went about fixing the car.

Satisfied she had made her point, Mona continued until she reached Pine Street. It wasn't long before she came upon a white house with one green shutter. The other houses were shutterless, so this had to be the one. Mona knocked on the torn screen door.

A thin girl with auburn hair came from the kitchen rubbing her hands on a dishtowel. She was wearing a limp, faded cotton dress, which looked a little tight around the waist and an apron. Although, she had been pretty at one time, her features had been ravaged by poverty, and she had the same hollowed-eyed expression as the rude man in the street. She noticed Mona's makeup, hat, and tidy brown suit. She immediately became suspicious. "What do you want?"

"Are you Clare?"

"Who might you be? Are you a church lady or selling something? I don't want to hear any silly sermons, and I don't have any money, so you best be going. I've got supper to fix."

Mona tried the screen door but it was locked. "Are you the Clare who was acquainted with Landis Garrett?"

Excited, Clare quickly unlocked and opened the screen door, pulling Mona inside. "You from Landis?"

"I'm sorry. No." Mona wondered if the girl knew Landis was dead. How could she not know?

"You're not one of his people?" The girl's face contorted as though Mona had taken all hope from her. She pulled her apron up and buried her face in it. Weeping, she darted into the kitchen.

Alarmed, Mona followed. "Oh, goodness. There, there now. Sit down, young lady. I'll make us some tea."

The girl pulled the apron away from her face and cried, "Got none. Got no coffee neither."

"How about a glass of water?" Mona asked, noticing an old fashioned hand pump at the sink.

"Well's out back. Pump don't work no more."

Mona pulled a handkerchief from her purse and handed it to the girl. "Are you Clare?"

Blowing her nose, the girl nodded.

"How old are you, dear?"

"Sixteen. I'll be seventeen the first of the new year," Clare said between sniffles.

"What's your last name?"

"O'Hara."

"And you knew Landis Garrett?"

Tears flowing from her eyes, she nodded. "Is you gonna put me in jail? I didn't mean to be a bad girl. He said it was all right as he was a deacon of the Baptist Church. He promised to help my daddy find a job."

"I think if anyone was going to jail, it would have been Landis. Not you." She glanced about the kitchen. Clare was cooking greens and looked like she was about to put cornbread batter into a hot skillet. Homemade lye soap bars were carefully lined up on a window sill. The room was shabby but tidy as was Clare's appearance before she started bawling. Mona took the skillet off the stove and laid it on the sink counter.

"Who are you? What do you want with me?"

"You were expecting someone connected with Landis Garrett?" Mona asked, ignoring Clare's questions.

"Did you bring me money? I was told someone was to bring money and a bus ticket."

"Were you to leave town?"

"Yes." Clare's bottom lip trembled.

"Who said they were bringing money?"

"Mrs. Garrett. Are you sure you're not Mrs. Garrett's secretary or something? You look awfully smart in that getup," Clare said, referring to Mona's modest suit.

"Why would Mrs. Garrett bring you money?"

Clare's cheeks turned bright red. "That's my business." Thinking for a moment, Clare grabbed Mona's hand. "Is you a special friend of Landis like I am?"

Mona noticed that Clare always spoke in the present tense when referring to Landis Garrett. "Were you?"

Clare nodded. "Much to my shame. Promises me money, but I never see a penny. Just bags of groceries from time to time, but not enough to really help us. No meat. Never any meat. Not even canned meat." Clare looked hopefully at

Mona. "Can you give me some money?"

"I need a few answers first."

"Who are you? Either tell me or be gone, Satan."

"I'm Mona Moon."

Clare drew back and pointed a finger at Mona. "You're the she-devil who's been tormenting my Landis. You get outta' my house."

"Clare, I've never tormented Landis nor am I responsible for his passing. Please listen to me."

Clare became agitated. "No. No. You get out of my daddy's house. I know what you did. The sheriff thinks you done kilt Landis."

"You've been talking to Monahan? He knows about you?"

Clare made a motion of turning a key in her mouth and throwing it away.

Mona realized Clare might be simple, but then again, she could be just starved, frightened, and confused. One thing was for certain, Mona's visit was causing the girl distress. "Clare, I'll leave after you tell me something. Are you in the family way?"

"Not supposed to tell. Not supposed to tell."

"Is Landis the father?"

Clare shook her head. "Mrs. Garrett said not to say nothing. She said I had to leave town."

Mona patted the girl's hand in sympathy and rose. "Thank you for talking with me, Clare." She glanced about the kitchen before making her escape. "I see that you have made a pan of lye soap," Mona said, referring to the bars curing on the windowsill. "Lye soap is so good for whites in the laundry."

"I made the soap myself."

"Would you sell me a few bars?"

Clare's eyes widened with the prospect of cash. "You got real money? No bartering now. I need real money."

Mona pulled a twenty dollar bill from her wallet and put in on the kitchen table. "I think this will cover the cost." Mona borrowed back the now damp handkerchief and wrapped four soap bars in it before storing the bundle in her purse. She bade Clare goodbye and hurried to her car.

Most people were inside now preparing supper, so Mona made a clean getaway without anyone seeing her leave Clare's house. Before she went back to her Daimler, Mona sidetracked back to the little store.

The clerk looked up and jumped to attention when he saw Mona enter. He quickly put out his cigarette and smiled, politely asking, "Did you find Clare?"

"Do the O'Hara's have an account here?"

"They have an account past due. No more credit for them."

"How much?"

The clerk looked in a small tin box and pulled out an index card. "Seven dollars and twelve cents."

Mona reached for her wallet. "I'll pay it, and I want you to deliver some groceries to the O'Hara's house after dark. Be discreet."

The clerk nodded and licked the end of a short pencil before he commenced to write.

Mona looked about the store. "A couple pounds of baloney. One of those country hams I see hanging. Two dozen eggs. Fresh now. No old eggs. Couple loaves of bread. Slice the bread first. Mustard. Ketchup. Salt. Pepper. Five pounds of potatoes. Two pounds of onions. A bottle of buttermilk."

"The O'Hara's got no icebox."

Mona didn't recall seeing a refrigerator. "Forget about the buttermilk. A tin of tea. A bag of coffee. Got any fruit?"

"Just canned fruit."

"A dozen assorted cans of fruit. A dozen cans of sweet milk. Couple jars of blackberry jam. A penny's worth of peppermint sticks. I see you have horehound candy. A penny's worth of that. Some rock candy. Throw in a dozen chocolate bars. Five pounds of flour, two pounds of sugar, and a tin of Calumet baking powder. A box of baking soda, too. Toothpaste powder and rose-scented cologne. That should about do it."

Excited, the clerk announced, "That comes to twenty-two dollars and fifty-four cents."

Mona gave him twenty-five dollars. "Put the change on their account."

"Yes, ma'am."

"Since we are such close friends now, I think we can be frank with each other. Did Landis Garrett ever come here?"

"Judge Garrett?" The clerk hesitated, pushing up his glasses.

"Quit stalling."

"Once or twice."

"What did he buy?"

The clerk scratched his head. "Mostly pork and beans. Maybe a sack of potatoes and greens. Cigarettes sometimes."

"Did he buy for himself or someone else?"

"He never said."

"Did you have suspicions?"

"Several men who don't live around these parts sometimes come in and purchase groceries."

"Like who?"

"You work for the paper?"

Mona smiled. "I'm not a reporter nor do I work for the police."

"I need to bite my tongue. I don't want to be found on a country lane with *my* head missing."

"Are you saying Judge Garrett knew something and that's what got him killed?"

"I think curiosity will get you killed just like a cat. You make no never mind."

Mona realized she had pushed the clerk as far as she could. "One more thing. You never saw me. Understand?"

The clerk, deciding to end the transaction on a friendly note, said, "I don't know who you are, lady, but I'm sure glad you stopped in my store and asked for directions."

"No one stopped in your store and asked for directions. No one paid off the O'Hara's account. You zeroed their account and took them groceries because you are a kind and generous man."

"I know how to keep my mouth shut . . . unlike some."

"Make sure you do. Good day to you, sir."

Mona left the store thinking the clerk knew more than he was saying. She also had a sinking feeling no good deed goes unpunished. Somehow buying groceries for Clare was going to come back to bite her in the tush.

Mona just knew it.

10

Several days later, Mona, Willie, and Dexter attended Landis Garrett's funeral together. Strength in numbers. As soon as Mona walked into the First Baptist Church, she could hear the tongues wagging. She smiled and greeted everyone politely. The best defense was a good offense. Mona knew most of the ladies would not rebuff her, but they would rip her apart privately like a terrier with a rat. Mona didn't really care as long as they treated her with respect in public. They wanted Mona to donate Moon money for their charities, so they would engage with her politely. Money did have its uses besides buying things. It gave one power.

The three of them got in the receiving line and waited for their turn to express their *heartfelt condolences* to Hazel Garrett.

If Hazel Garrett was startled to see Mona and the Deatherages, she didn't show it. "Nice of you to come."

"I want you to know everyone who works with Mooncrest Enterprises is doing their utmost to cooperate with the police," Dexter assured.

Willie clutched Hazel's hand. "It's a terrible tragedy." When Hazel didn't respond, Willie said in an obligatory manner, "You must call me if you need something."

"Thank you. I will."

Mona remained silent until Hazel cast her eyes upon her. "Very sorry for your loss, Hazel."

"Are you?"

Mona was not about to get into an argument with Hazel standing by the closed casket of her dead husband. "I hope the culprit is caught soon. My condolences on the loss of your husband."

Determined to embarrass Mona, Hazel spoke loudly, "It would seem that you would be glad to see Landis dead."

Mona angrily turned her back so others waiting in the receiving line couldn't overhear her words. "Perhaps you would like to discuss Clare

O'Hara here and now. Is she a motive for murder?"

Hazel looked astonished but recovered quickly. "I don't know a Clare O'Hara."

"She's waiting for money you promised. Whose baby is she carrying?"

Looking about, Hazel pleaded, "Don't make a scene, please."

"Then smile and thank me for coming."

Hazel clasped Mona's hand. "Thank you so much for coming, Mona. It's been a terrible ordeal for both of us."

Mona nodded *sadly* and followed the Deatherages to a pew in the back.

"That was some great acting with Hazel. I really believed you were actually distressed to see the old fuss bucket die," Willie whispered.

Dexter added, "I think Hazel wins the acting award for playing the grieving widow, God bless her. However, she'll brighten up once she gets her hands on all that money. I think Landis held on to the first nickel he ever made."

"How would you know how much money Landis had? Judges don't make much," Mona commented.

Dexter sniffed. "Judges are paid better than ninety percent of the rest of the men in this state. Besides, judges like Landis always have ways of filling their coffers."

Willie slid a flask out of her purse. "You mean bribery, dear?"

Dexter looked askance at Willie sipping from her flask. "Not here, Wilhelmina. It's unseemly."

She handed the flask to him. "It's tea. I get parched nowadays. I need my liquids."

Dexter hissed, "Put the flask away before anyone sees you, honey. Next time carry a thermos with you."

Mona was disappointed Willie wasn't carrying bootlegged bourbon this time. She could have used a snort. "Let's get back to the bribery angle."

"He was ruthless in the courtroom. If the defendant was poor, or worse, poor and black, boom, he'd give them the whammy. Landis was unnecessarily harsh in his sentencing. I thought he should have been removed from the bench years ago. He was not impartial to those he thought socially inferior," Dexter said.

"So, some of my staff tell me. It seems many

of my farm workers were thrown into jail by Landis Garrett for petty offenses."

"If one of our Moon men was arrested for public intoxication, Landis would make him serve three days in jail or pay a huge fine instead of letting him sleep it off overnight in the jail like most judges would do. People hated his guts. Personally, I thought the man odious," Dexter said.

"Perhaps an honest judge will be elected now," Mona said, adjusting her black hat.

Dexter scoffed, "In this town? It was rumored Garrett was on the take, and Sheriff Monahan was in his back pocket. It was never proven because both men were slicker than okra."

"Things are improving," Willie suggested. She could see Dexter was working himself into a tizzy. Her conservative husband was actually a reformer at heart and hated men like Garrett, who gave the law a bad name and corrupted justice.

"I hope President Roosevelt really shakes things up, and the conniving backroom politics stop." Tired, Dexter sighed and pulled out his pocket watch. "I wish they'd get this show on the road. I've got things to do today."

Noting that Dexter was in a very talkative mood, Mona asked, "What about his women? Was Landis Garrett always a masher?" She wanted to hear Dexter's take on this subject, but Willie spoke up.

Willie confided, "He was always putting a move on someone in our social group. Usually, the wives just laughed it off, but I heard Landis got rough with a couple of them."

"You mean he forced himself?" Mona asked, incredulously.

"Nothing that serious. Stealing a kiss, now and then. Pushing women into a corner and taking liberties with his hands. The women would tell their husbands who would have a quiet talk with Landis, usually with their fists, and that would end it. Landis would always push to see how far he could get away with things."

"Disgusting," Dexter said, with a fierce look on his face.

Mona smiled inwardly, knowing that if a woman made a pass at Dexter, he'd faint from sheer outrage. He was such a boy scout.

"Then why is everyone acting like his death is

a big loss?"

"Because this is the South, my dear. Appearances are everything. Half the people here had a bone to pick with Landis. Some are coming to see Hazel through her time of grief. Some are coming because they're nosy and want to see who is here, and others are coming to make sure Landis is, in fact, really dead," Willie explained.

"But you better believe that all of them are here to see if you would show and observe your interaction with Hazel," Dexter added.

"Glad both of you came with me. Otherwise, I would have had to walk in by myself feeling like Daniel in the lions' den."

Two men in their twenties sidled up to Hazel, spoke a few words, escorted her to the front pew, and sat beside her.

Willie leaned over. "Those are Hazel's two boys. There is a third child. A girl, but I don't see her."

"They don't look too broken up," Dexter said out of the corner of his mouth.

"They both disowned Landis. I don't believe either one of the boys has spoken to him for over a year."

ABIGAIL KEAM

Mona asked, "Both at the same time?"

"Yes. I got the information from Hazel's sister, Louella, when it happened. She said Hazel was all broken up about it."

"What was it about?"

"I don't know, Mona. Neither did Louella. Hazel wouldn't say."

"Hmm," Mona said. "Events surrounding Landis get more and more curious."

"Hush now, both of you. Preacher's getting ready to speak," Dexter admonished.

Mona sat quietly lost in her own thoughts. She wondered if the blowup with the sons had to do with the discovery of Judge Garrett's relationship with Clare O'Hara. And where was the daughter? Something seemed very wrong in the Garrett household. Mona suddenly felt unclean, but she dare not walk out. It would be considered disrespectful and an affront. Mona almost laughed out loud. If she had tried to leave, Dexter would probably pull Mona back into her seat and tell her to behave.

She heard the doors at the rear of the sanctuary open, and a wave of cool air drifted throughout the church. Hearing the pew behind her groan with great weight suddenly thrust upon it, Mona sniffed and smelled the cologne Sheriff Monahan used. The mere thought of Monahan sitting behind her was deeply disconcerting. Mona always liked to see her enemies and having her back exposed to him made her uneasy. The phrase *knife in the back* wasn't just a slogan.

"Let us pray," the preacher said. Everyone bowed their heads as the preacher mumbled some generic prayer. Relieved the preacher spoke briefly, Mona put on her gloves to leave, but then he asked if anyone wanted to speak. She watched the crowd stir, but no one got up and spoke on the behalf of Landis Garrett.

The silence became deafening until the elder of the two sons got up and drawled in a heavy Southern accent, "My family thanks you for coming. We appreciate your heartfelt condolences and offers of support. This concludes the public portion of the funeral. The family will be accompanying my father to the Lexington Cemetery for a private ceremony and burial. Again, thank you for coming." He motioned for the organist to play *The Old Rugged Cross,* a favorite hymn of Baptists.

Mona jumped to her feet and tugged on Willie's sleeve. "Let's go."

"What's your hurry, Miss Mona?" Sheriff Monahan asked, stepping in front and tipping the bill of his Stetson to the women.

"I didn't know you were behind us," Willie lied. "What did you think about the service?"

"Nice as they go, but brief, don't you think?"

"Perhaps that's something to ponder upon, Sheriff," Mona said, looking up at Monahan. He was a big man, both in height and girth. She sized him up, knowing she would never win a tussle with him. There was a great deal of fat on the sheriff, but lots of muscle underneath it.

"What do you mean?"

"No one spoke on Garrett's behalf. Not even his children. Don't lawmen usually start with the family when someone is murdered, especially if the family wasn't sorry to see the deceased dead?"

"What are you suggesting?"

"There was trouble in the Garrett household. Hazel was estranged as were Garrett's children. I understand the sons hadn't spoken to him in over a year." Mona turned around and surveyed the people leaving. "And where is Garrett's daughter?"

Willie nervously poked Mona in the back.

"What did the autopsy say? It would be helpful if you knew when Garrett was killed. It's my guess the coroner couldn't place exact time of death due to the damage caused by the river. He can estimate within a day or so, but that's all, and that really opens up the pool of suspects. It could be anyone in this church for instance." Mona said, ignoring Willie's continued poking in her back.

"Or I could be looking at her," Monahan said, looking down at Mona.

Mona laughed. "You've been watching too many James Cagney films. I don't need to kill anyone. I get what I want using the law, and I usually win because I'm usually right. At least I was with Landis Garrett, and the courts backed me up every step of the way. Nice to see you again. Good day."

Willie and Dexter bade the sheriff a good day and followed Mona out of the church where Willie lit into her. "I told you that information about Hazel's sons in confidence. I have no idea what I'm going to say to Louella if this gets back to her."

"You didn't make it clear it was a confidential matter."

Willie sniffed. "Well, it was, honey. Now I know better than to tell you any secrets."

"*I tell secrets!* Oh, Willie, you take the cake," Mona huffed, pulling Willie along with her to the Daimler. She hurried them into the car and instructed Jamison to make haste. Willie was having several couples over to dinner that evening and needed to start a pot roast, while Dexter had to get back to the office.

Forty minutes later Mona was climbing out of the Daimler, but neither Thomas, Samuel, nor Chloe greeted her at the door. One or the other always met her at the front door because Burl, the gatehouse guard, would call Moon Manor and alert them. Mona shot Jamison a look of concern. "That's odd."

"You want me to go inside with you, Miss Mona?"

"No thank you, Jamison. You go on. The Pinkertons are still here. I'll be safe." Mona marched up the front steps and asked one of the Pinkertons guarding the portico, "Do you know where Thomas or Samuel are?"

"They're probably in the kitchen, Miss."

"Why is that?"

"There was a problem in town."

"What happened?"

"We don't have the details yet. Better check inside."

"I see." Mona took out her door key and unlocked the front door, slamming it shut, and locking it behind her. "Thomas!" she called out, but no sign of him. And where was Chloe? She always greeted Mona, wagging her tail, and wanting to be petted.

Lightly muted noises sounded from the back of the house so Mona threw her hat and purse on the hallway side table before rushing to the kitchen. As she entered Monsieur Bisaillon's domain, she saw a clump of people huddled before a massive harvest table. "What's going on?" Mona asked sharply.

The huddle, consisting of Violet, Jetta, Thomas, and Samuel, parted so Mona could see Monsieur Bisaillon and Kenesaw Mountain tending to Obadiah and Jedediah with iodine and bandages. Their faces were battered and swollen, their shirts had been ripped, and blood stained their clothes.

"My God!" Mona gasped. "What happened?"

"They got jumped by five white boys when they went into town," Kenesaw muttered, mopping blood off Jedediah's brow.

Almost in tears, Monsieur Bisaillon blurted out, "I needed turmeric for tonight's dish, so I asked them to go to the store with me. When we left the store, these five thugs jumped us and beat the daylights out of Obbie and Jed while two held me back. When they got finished with them, one of them says to me, 'This is what will happen to you, Froggie, if you keep working for the Moons.'"

"Didn't anyone help?"

"Not a soul but Jed and Obbie gave as good as they got."

Mona studied the wounds on the two young men. The cuts and bruises looked nasty but not life threatening. "I'm so sorry. I'll call the law and have those miscreants thrown in jail."

Jed held a towel filled with ice to his left eye. "We've never had trouble before. Doesn't seem right." He shook his head and seemed shaken.

"Can you identify them?" Mona asked.

Obbie spoke up, "I knew three of them. I don't know who the other two were."

Jedediah shot Obadiah a hateful glance. "Be quiet, Obbie. You don't know nothing."

Obadiah lowered his head and wouldn't make eye contact with Mona when she asked him further questions.

Seeing the two young men were reluctant to speak, Mona turned to Kenesaw. "Call the doctor please, and have him come straight here. I dare not take these lads to the hospital when feelings are running so high. I'll let the doctor make the decision about their care."

"No, Miss Moon. Don't," Obadiah begged. "The doctor won't do nothing, no way."

"We'll see about that. Make the call, Kenesaw."

Kenesaw went to the newly installed phone on the wall and called Doctor Tuttle. The doctor was not in, so Kenesaw left a message with his housekeeper. Then he called Dexter speaking quietly so Mona wouldn't hear. After a brief conversation, he hung up the phone.

"Miss Mona, may I speak with you?" Kenesaw asked as Mona washed blood from a kitchen rag in the new sink.

"Of course," Mona said. She glanced back at Jetta and Violet who were cutting off Obbie and Jed's tattered shirts, while Samuel stood by with two of his shirts the young men could borrow.

"Let's step in here," Kenesaw suggested, opening the door to the laundry room.

Mona followed, wondering what her farm manager was going to say.

Kenesaw shut the door softly and paused, trying to determine how he was going to speak his peace.

"Spit it out, Kenesaw. You've got something on your mind."

Kenesaw's face took on a mournful expression. "You must stop."

"What do you mean?"

"This needs to be kept quiet. Do not report the assault to the police."

"But Obbie and Jed were attacked in broad daylight. Steps need to be taken."

"It's a trap, don't you see? The sheriff wants you to report it so he can make Obbie and Jed's lives miserable. By the time he'd get finished with them, it will be Obadiah and Jedediah who attacked those city boys."

"This happened in Lexington. Monahan has no jurisdiction there."

"Monahan and the police chief are thick as thieves. The police chief will do whatever Monahan wants. Can't you see that? Count your blessings, Miss Mona. They only got thumped. No broken bones. No stab wounds. Their pride is hurt more than anything else. You drop this, you hear."

"I don't like men giving me orders, Mr. Mountain."

"Miss Mona, I'm not giving you any orders. I'm talking common sense. You're from the North. Things work differently down here, and it's not always gentle. Obadiah and Jedediah were beaten up because they're young, black, and work for you. The next time they strike it might be one of our women, and what they do to her will be a lot worse than what they did to those young men. They'll make an example of her by cutting off her hair, ripping her clothes to shreds—maybe slicing up her face with a dull knife besides a beating. It's been done before to make a point. Would you like to see that happen to Violet or Jetta?"

Mona gasped, "Don't even say such a thing." She threw up her hands. "What am I to do? My employees can't stay prisoners on this farm."

"Everyone needs to sit tight until either the sheriff gives up on you or the real culprit is caught."

"All right, Kenesaw. I'll have a talk with Mr. Deatherage about what to do and take it from there."

"Now, you're using your head."

Mona didn't like Kenesaw's condescension but realized he was only trying to help. She would deal with him later. Right now she wanted to tend to Obbie and Jed.

Where was that doctor?

11

By late afternoon Doctor Tuttle arrived and tended to Obbie and Jed. Everyone was relieved when he said they could recuperate at their mother's house. Mona made the doctor promise to check on them every day until they returned to work which would be in a few days or so.

Monsieur Bisaillon tendered his resignation but relented when Mona offered a fifty dollar bonus and new curtains for his quarters. Pacified, the cook related he was serving cold cuts for dinner, and no one better complain.

Meanwhile, Mooncrest Farm had been put on lockdown. The perimeters were patrolled by the Pinkertons. All guests and trades people had to sign in when entering and sign out when leaving by the main gate. Mr. Deatherage bought Burl a

Kodak Brownie camera so he could photograph any unknown person entering Mooncrest Farm.

It was the gloaming of the day when Mona looked up from her desk as Jetta handed her another message from Dexter Deatherage. "What now?" Mona asked, reading the note. "I was hoping things were settling down."

"Things will look brighter in the morning," Jetta offered.

"Always the optimist, huh, Jetta," Mona said, tidying up her desk.

"Monsieur Bisaillon has put out ham sandwiches in the dining room with some hot cider and lemon sponge cake. I'm afraid the sponge cake looks rather old. It makes a hollow sound when you tap on it. I'm not going to eat it."

"Did you notice our French cook lost his accent during his telling of the attack?"

Jetta smirked. "That's because Bisaillon is really an Italian from New Jersey."

"Figures."

"Any answer for Mr. Deatherage?"

"Call his secretary and say yes."

"That's all?"

"Quite." Mona glanced at Chloe's empty bed

near her desk. "I haven't seen Chloe since I got back. Where is she?"

"Well, I don't know. She was in the house, but with all the excitement, I guess everyone lost track of her."

Concerned, Mona asked, "Can you and Violet search the upstairs for her? I'll have Samuel and Thomas look downstairs."

"She's probably pouting in a corner somewhere because no one is paying any attention to her."

"All the ruckus might have frightened her. I hope she didn't sneak outside when a door was opened. I've always feared some of Garrett's men would throw poisoned meat over the fence for her to eat."

"Don't worry. We'll find her," Jetta assured, knowing Mona had grown quite fond of the standard poodle.

Mona walked out to the portico and asked the guards, "Have either of you seen a white dog. A poodle?"

The red-headed guard answered, "She ran out when they brought those kitchen workers home."

"Did she come back?"

"Not that we saw."

"Which way did she go?"

"That way," the guard pointed toward the north side of the farm.

Mona rushed down the steps.

Jetta called to her. "Miss, come back. It's getting dark. Mr. Deatherage doesn't want anyone wandering around the estate after the sun sets."

"I'll be quick. I need to find my dog," Mona called over her shoulder as she hurried across the driveway and toward the nearest pasture. She climbed over the fence and wandered through one pasture and the next calling Chloe's name.

Curious foals followed Mona with several nipping her clothes, while others ran to their mothers when she spoke to them.

Stable workers, holding flashlights or kerosene lamps, whistled to gather the horses to the barns. They waved to Mona but did not approach her. She called out, asking if they had seen Chloe. They yelled back they hadn't seen her.

Frustrated, Mona kept going until she was at the property line between her estate and Lord Farley's. Leaning against a fence post, Mona wondered about Robert Farley. She guessed he was married to Lady Alice by now. Depressed by that thought, Mona pushed away from the fence and gave out one last call for Chloe before heading back home.

After turning toward Moon Manor, Mona heard barking in the distance. She listened in the dark. It certainly sounded like Chloe. Determined, Mona climbed the fence and rushed through the field toward Farley's house. As she got closer, Mona was sure it was Chloe barking. Why was Chloe at Farley's house? "Chloe? Chloe! Chloe! Come, girl! Come!"

Rushing up the pathway to the mansion's formal garden and through the gate to the swimming pool area, Mona realized the lights were on at Farley's house. She didn't stop to think what that might mean.

She caught sight of Chloe about a hundred feet away and noticed a man hidden in the shadows doling out treats for Chloe to jump up and snatch. The man laughed as he bent over to pet the dog.

"Chloe!" Mona scolded.

The silhouetted figure froze for a second and then stepped into the light. "Hello, Mona. I was hoping you would come."

12

"Robert!" Mona cried, startled. She took a step back.

Chloe ran over and jumped up on Mona.

"So, this is where you went to. Down, girl. Down."

Chloe reluctantly sat and whimpered.

Mona scratched Chloe behind the ears playing for time. She was stunned at the sight of seeing Robert Farley and didn't know what to say.

"She seems awfully excited," Lord Farley said.

"We had a bit of a ruckus this afternoon. Must have frightened her," Mona said, discreetly looking at Farley's ring finger. No wedding band. Hmm.

"Ruckus? What kind of ruckus?"

"Nothing. It's settled. We'll be going now.

Thank you for finding her."

"Wait a moment. We haven't seen each other for months. Please stay."

"I need to get back."

"I was just having a drink by the pool. Join me."

"No. We really must be going."

"Let me walk you back."

"That won't be necessary, really."

"I insist, Mona." Lord Farley strode over to the gate and opened it. "Ladies first."

Mona swept through while Chloe shot past, leaving her alone with His Lordship.

"Chloe will be all right. She'll circle back to us." Farley extended his arm to Mona.

Mona reluctantly took hold of it. Touching Farley brought back feelings Mona wanted to keep submerged, but she couldn't deny seeing him again made her heart beat faster. "How did you find Chloe?" she said, trying to keep her voice even.

"I didn't. Chloe found me. She scratched at the gate."

"Oh."

"I phoned Moon Manor, but they said you

were out. I figured you were looking for her."

"Oh." Mona winced, thinking she was sounding like a simpleton. Was "oh" all she could think of to say?

Farley stopped suddenly and turned to face Mona, grabbing her around the waist. "Why didn't you write to me, Mona? I wrote to you every week, but never heard from you."

"What was there to say? You have your life in England, and I have my life here."

"For four months not a peep from you."

"I thought it best."

"Did you even read my letters?"

"They were full of information about how your father was doing, the changes taking place at Bosworth Manor, and witty observations about the dinner parties you attended."

"Alice said you never answered her letters either."

Mona said nothing.

"I even tried calling several times, but you were always out."

"Been busy. I was told about your calls."

"But you never called back. Why?"

"I think you know why."

Farley pulled Mona closer.

"Don't," Mona said, pushing against him.

But Farley overpowered her and pulled her close, pressing his cheek against Mona's. "I missed you, dearest. Deeply missed you."

Mona inhaled Farley's masculine scent and cologne. Against her better judgment, she yielded and leaned into him. He felt wonderful—he felt like home.

Farley kissed the top of her head and then lifted her chin. "You have no idea how often I thought of you and of doing this." He kissed Mona passionately, pressing tighter against her.

Could it be this simple? Farley was home, and he wanted her. Maybe even loved her? Could it really be this simple? Mona didn't think so. She finally pulled away, breaking out of his arms.

Farley looked hurt. "Mona?"

"Why are you here, Robert?"

"I wanted to see you. I missed you. I told you in England I had feelings for you."

"Really? Then why were there pictures of you dilly-dallying with beautiful women splashed all over the society pages? Even in the backwater of Kentucky we got news about your going-ons."

Farley displayed a self-satisfied grin. "Ah, so that's it. You're jealous."

"I am not," Mona denied, stubbornly.

"I never had dalliances with anyone. Those were married friends who needed an escort to various functions."

"Married! When did that ever stop you?"

Farley laughed. "You *are* jealous. That's grand. It means I'm making progress. You like me, Mona Moon. You think I'm the cat's meow."

"Go to the Devil," Mona huffed, stomping off. She was embarrassed. Every time she had read about him in the paper with some woman, it tore at her heart. Now he was home mocking her tender feelings.

Still laughing, Farley called after her. "I'll be over tomorrow, Mona. We've got lots to talk about. Good night dearest Mona Moon."

Mona wanted to turn around and slap Farley's face, but she wouldn't give him the pleasure of letting him know how angry she was. It would only prove him right.

She was jealous. Seriously jealous. The problem was Mona realized she loved Farley, but did he feel the same? Was pursuing her merely sport for him? She didn't want her heart broken like he had broken Alice's heart. It almost ruined her.

Oh, why did Lawrence Robert Emerton Dagobert Farley have to come back?

What was Mona going to do about him?

13

Mona didn't have much time to dwell upon Robert Farley, Marquess of Gower. The next morning Monahan showed up with another warrant to search the barns and outbuildings on all four thousand acres. Using her desk phone, Mona told Burl to let the sheriff and his men through the gates, and then she called Dexter.

Assured that Dexter would handle any and all problems, Mona went to work. She and Jetta went over the day's schedule and then retired to the verandah where they had a light morning repast as Mona perused the mail.

Both women turned when the verandah door opened and Lord Farley stepped through with Violet, grinning from ear to ear. Chloe trailed behind.

Jetta uttered, "Oh, my Lord." She quickly jumped up and curtsied.

"To which lord are you referring?" Mona asked, rolling her eyes and thinking the two young women were acting daffy.

Farley bowed. "Good morning, beautiful ones, and I say that with the greatest respect."

"Good morning, Lord Farley," Violet and Jetta sang in unison.

"How is Miss Madeline Mona on this glorious morning?" he asked.

"Busy."

Farley grabbed the mail from Mona's hands. "Too pretty a day to be working. Let's go for a ride and look at the trees. It's the peak of their fall color. What do you think, ladies? Shouldn't Miss Mona take the day off?"

"I think it's a splendid idea," Jetta agreed, ignoring the hateful look Mona shot her way. "She works much too hard. The morning off would do Miss Mona good."

Farley swung Mona's chair around and pulled her to her feet. "Your betters have spoken. Grab a sweater and let's be off. My chariot awaits."

Farley's lively banter was infectious, and Mona

caught herself laughing. "All right. All right. But I need to be back by lunch. I've got gobs of work to do."

"Gobs?" Farley said making a funny face to Violet and Jetta. "Must be serious then. Shall we call a doctor?"

"I shan't go unless you promise to bring me back by one-thirty," Mona insisted.

"Let's hit the road then."

Before Mona had a chance to move, Chloe turned toward the house and snarled, baring her teeth.

Jetta and Violet stood back from her.

"What's she going on about?" Farley asked. He had never seen the dog act this way.

"She's frightened," Violet said. "She snarled the same way the night that Master Manfred died."

Mona bent over and petted Chloe. "What's the matter, girl?"

Chloe turned and licked Mona's hand, only to return to her defensive snarling stance a second later.

Mona stood quickly when a ruckus was heard in the manor.

With movement catching their eyes, everyone looked through the windows and saw Thomas and Samuel trying to bar Monahan and his men from approaching the verandah.

Farley threw open the verandah glass doors and snapped, "What's going on here?"

Breathless, Thomas explained, "Sorry. We tried to keep them out, but they barged right in."

"It's fine, Thomas. You and Samuel may leave," Mona said.

"No, Miss Mona," Thomas said stubbornly.

Sheriff Monahan roughly pushed Thomas aside, almost knocking him down. He and a couple of his men stepped out on the verandah.

Violet ran over to Thomas to help steady him.

Farley stepped in front of Monahan. "Try doing that to me, Sheriff."

"I have no quarrel with you, Farley. Step aside."

"What if I don't? You going to knock me down like you did that old man?" Farley leaned in and looked Monahan squarely in the face. "There's a name for men who do such things."

Monahan's eyes widened. He was shocked that even a man like Farley with his power would dare confront him. "This is official business. Stay out of it."

"What if I make it my business?"

Mona put her hand on Farley's arm. "Thank you. I'll take it from here, but I would appreciate it if you would stay and witness."

"Wild horses couldn't drag me away."

"Jetta, would you please transcribe my interaction with our dear sheriff. Every word, exactly. Note that he purposely shoved my butler aside. Violet, will you take Chloe to the kitchen. I'm afraid she might bite someone in all of this undue excitement."

Trembling, Violet grabbed Chloe's collar and pulled her along to the kitchen while giving Monahan a dirty look.

Clasping her hands, Mona turned to Monahan. "Now, why all this fuss?"

"Do you know anything about this?" Monahan held up a hatchet stained with dried blood and matted hair.

Mona angrily took a deep breath, wanting to answer calmly. "I've never seen that hatchet before in my life."

"There's a farm worker saying otherwise."

"Then he is lying. What would I be doing with a hatchet?"

"Perhaps chopping off the head of Landis Garrett."

Farley guffawed. "Don't be absurd. A cattywampus accusation, if ever I heard one."

"This farm worker says he saw me cut off Garrett's head?"

"He said he saw you working with this hatchet."

"Doing what?"

"Splitting wood."

"I can assure that I have never touched firewood since I've been to Moon Manor."

Farley interrupted. "You said farm worker. One of Mooncrest Farm's workers?"

Monahan hesitated for a moment. "One of Judge Garrett's men tipped us off."

Mona and Farley burst out laughing.

Farley asked, "Did he tell you where to find it?"

"Of course, he did," Mona said.

"How much did he get paid for concocting this absurd fantasy?" Farley accused. "Even if Mona's fingerprints are on it, there's the problem of a hundred and twenty pound woman subduing a man who was over six feet tall and weighed two hundred pounds."

"Regardless, we have a witness who saw Miss Mona with the supposed murder weapon. I'm sorry, Miss, but we have to take you down to get your fingerprints on record."

"Who's this *witness*?"

"It was an anonymous tip."

Farley said, "He wouldn't give his name, but said he worked for the Garretts? This has all the hallmarks of a set up to frame me."

Monahan stepped forward to take Mona into custody, but Farley pushed Mona out of reach behind him. "Where did you find this hatchet?"

"Buried in the dirt floor of the Moon Manor smokehouse."

"Did it ever occur to you, Monahan, this *tipster* might have killed Judge Garrett and planted the body and this hatchet on Miss Mona's property?"

"Regardless, I still got to take her fingerprints. It's my job."

"There is no need to take Miss Mona into custody. I will bring her in myself this afternoon. That will give you time to check to see if there are any fingerprints on the hatchet. I think you will agree that if no fingerprints are found on the weapon, Miss Mona will not have to be finger-printed herself."

Monahan pulled on his earlobe, thinking.

Farley warned Monahan. "Mona Moon is not some field hand you can rough up and get a confession. If there are no fingerprints on that hatchet, and you pursue this with her, there will be grave consequences. I'll call Governor Laffoon myself about your harassment."

Knowing Farley could make serious trouble for him, Monahan relented. "Very well. I guess there's no use parading Miss Mona downtown in handcuffs. She can come in voluntarily like you said." He looked at Mona. "Don't make me come get you now, ya hear?"

"You'll always know where I am, Sheriff. Thomas and Samuel, will you show Sheriff Monahan and his men out, please?"

"With pleasure, Miss," Thomas said, straightening his vest and jacket.

Monahan pushed Thomas again on his way out as if to make a final point.

Samuel followed to make sure they left the

house and to see what happened to the Pinkerton guards.

Jetta followed Thomas into the kitchen and poured him a cup of coffee, saying nothing. What was there to say? The poor and those not among the ruling class got pushed around. That was the way it was in Lexington, and those who tried to change things found themselves on the wrong side of the law.

Jetta couldn't think but that Mona had been warned.

Now there would be hell to pay.

14

Farley sat down and took out a gold cigarette case, offering one to Mona.

"You know I don't smoke."

"Nervous habit," he replied, tapping the end of a cigarette on the case. "Perhaps you should get Lizzie Borden to autograph the hatchet."

"She's dead."

"Not the point, my sweet American cow."

"You didn't have to save me. I could have handled the situation myself."

"Really? How's that? Thrown into a paddy wagon and jostling about with a bunch of rough men. You needed me. Why don't you just admit I was here in the nick of time?"

Mona shook her head in disbelief. "If you could hear yourself. You are such a popinjay."

"The thing is Monahan knows you didn't have anything to do with Garrett's death. He just wants to intimidate you."

Mona sat down beside him and poured herself a cup of coffee. "There are other reformers in this town. I don't know why he's picking on me."

"It should be obvious. You're a woman . . . alone. You let your miners unionize. Other bigwigs see this as a serious threat and worry that the workers at their businesses will want to unionize as well."

"Even when I can prove production is up? Happy workers mean larger profits."

"Mona, you don't get it. It's not about profits. It's about power. Unions mean loss of dominance for the owners. Money is only secondary to these men. It's the ability to control their environment which drives them."

"Then the money?"

Farley nodded. "Then the money. Unions mean larger wages for the workers and less dough for management to stick in their pockets."

"Well, I know my fingerprints are not on that hatchet. I've never seen it before."

"Doesn't matter. Monahan will come up with

something else to make your life miserable."

"Obviously, the farmhand was mistaken."

"Obviously, there is no farmhand. Mona, darling, I think you should take this seriously."

Mona took a sip of coffee and put the cup down. "Where were those Pinkerton guards when I needed them?"

Farley picked up his cup and drank the rest of the coffee. "Probably held at gunpoint by Monahan's men. Don't let Monahan on your property again if you can help it."

"Who do you think killed Garrett?"

Farley ran a thumb across his chin. "I would start with the family first."

"Exactly. The sons were estranged from the father. I think I know why, but I need to be sure. Before you take me to the Sheriff's office, can you drop me by Hazel Garrett's apartment?"

"Just walk across the field. My maid told me Hazel has taken up residence again in the Garrett family home. In fact, she gave me the entire rundown concerning the bazaar drama about Garrett's murder up till today."

"It's amazing how our employees know more about what's going on than we do. Does she know anything about Garrett's daughter?"

"No, but I bet your Aunt Melanie does."

Mona grimaced. "I need to talk with dear old Aunt Melanie. She's been breaking her contract with Mooncrest Enterprises."

"You mean by badmouthing you around town?"

"Your maid again?" Mona asked, looking frazzled.

Farley nodded. "I wouldn't take it to heart. Everyone considers Melanie a little wackadoodle." He reached over and clasped Mona's hand. "May we talk about something else? The reason I wanted to take you on a drive was to talk with you privately. I need to discuss a matter of some importance."

"Can't it wait? I've got so much on my mind."

"I don't think so."

Mona sighed. "What is it then?"

Farley began to speak when Violet poked her head out through the verandah doors. "Miss Mona, Mr. Deatherage is here and waiting in your office."

Mona stood. "I'm sorry, Robert. Whatever you were going to tell me will have to wait."

Farley stood as well and walked with Mona back into the manor. "I'll be back to take you to the sheriff's office."

Mona walked Farley out. "Hopefully, it won't come to that. I'm sure it's what Dexter wants to talk about with me."

"Regardless, I'll be back. I really need to speak with you, Mona."

"This afternoon, then."

"Shake on it," Farley said, thrusting out his hand.

Mona laughed and shook hands.

"Remember, you shook on it." Farley gave her a quick peck on the cheek before taking his leave. "See you in a few hours."

Samuel showed up out of nowhere to escort Farley out. He must have been listening through the ductwork again in order to know Farley was leaving. She shook her head in disbelief, knowing she had instructed the general contractor to fix that particular idiosyncrasy at Moon Manor so the staff couldn't benevolently spy on her. Obviously, it had not been fixed.

Mona would think about it later. At the moment her mind was fixed on what Farley wanted to tell her. She hoped it wasn't news that would make her cry.

She had cried over him enough in the past few months.

Mona didn't want to give Lawrence Robert Emerton Dagobert Farley another one of her tears.

No man was worth that.

15

After meeting with Dexter, Mona sneaked past the guards through the kitchen and walked along the service roads until she came to a limestone stacked rock wall standing between her property and the Garrett's. The locals called these types of dry stacked walls—slave walls. Originally built by the Irish and then by slaves, these walls dotted the Bluegrass landscape. Mona knew the wall was very old as moss covered the stones and there were deep pits in the rock surfaces exposed to the weather.

A wooden stile was built on both sides of the wall, making it easy to climb over. Obviously, the owners of the two farms had been on friendly terms at one time. Farm owners also shared workers and these types of fence ladders made it easy for workers to move from one farm to the other. It certainly made it possible for a bribed worker or one of Landis' kinfolk to move between the two farms to plant a bloody hatchet.

Mona easily climbed the stile and meandered toward the Garrett home. She wasn't sure what she was going to say, but hopefully she would find some answers. Even a crumb of information would be helpful because Mona was currently stumbling in the dark as to who killed Landis.

Luckily, Mona spied Hazel working in the garden cutting flowers for an arrangement. She was wearing a flowered cotton day dress with a big floppy hat to protect her alabaster skin. Thick cotton gloves protected Hazel's hands as she hummed *The Ballad of Barbara Ellen.*

Mona walked up behind her. "Hazel."

Startled, Hazel swirled around with a pair of scissors held in her left hand and a basket of flowers in her right.

Mona took a step back.

"Goodness! You startled me."

Mona said, "I'm sorry. I came over to see if you needed anything."

"What would I need from you?"

"Perhaps a kind word."

"I know what I need. You should turn yourself in as the murderer of my husband. Sheriff Monahan was over here and told me about finding the ax which killed my husband in your smokehouse."

"Hazel, I didn't come over here to fight. You know it was someone in your employment who buried a hatchet and then told Monahan where to find it. The finger of culpability is pointed at you. Not me. My lawyer tells me he can make a good case of suing your estate if the harassment doesn't stop."

"I had nothing to do with my husband's death, but I can tell you I'm not sorry."

"Who tipped off the sheriff, Hazel?"

"I don't know, Mona, and that's the truth."

"Somebody close to you is trying to make it look like Mooncrest Enterprises is responsible for your husband's demise."

"I think it is you personally who is being targeted."

"Did it ever occur to you that you might be in danger?"

Hazel gestured with the scissors. "Why me?

I've done nothing."

"The murderer might think you know something that Landis did or held sway over someone. Might be about money. Who knows."

"Are you threatening me?"

"I'm suggesting you need to be careful."

"I would like you to leave."

"Not before I have some answers. Again, I want to know if your sons knew about Clare O'Hara?"

Hazel gazed toward the house. "My sons are home. I don't want you stirring up mischief about Clare."

"Is that what the estrangement was about?"

Hazel nodded slightly. "They are scared stiff the truth will come out, and the family will be disgraced. Both are lawyers, and my oldest wants to be a judge. If this scandal got into the papers, his chances of being elected as a judge are nil."

"Hazel, I know you talked with Clare and offered her money."

"Yes! To get out of town and start a new life. All she has to do is sign a piece of paper stating that Landis is not the father of her child, and she will get it."

"But she won't sign it?"

"The little fool says part of Landis' estate is hers because of the child. My God, Mona, she loved the man. Can you imagine anyone loving Landis? I couldn't make her understand Landis had done this before. Clare was not the first peccadillo of his, and if he had lived, she wouldn't have been the last. Who knows how many of his little bastards are running around town?"

"Clare is sixteen. She said Landis promised her family money if she let him sleep with her. I don't call Clare's behavior as that of a vixen. I call her behavior as one desperate to survive. Landis was truly despicable to use a girl's hunger to get into her bloomers."

"I'm not disagreeing with you, Mona. Like I said, I'm not sorry to see Landis dead."

"The Jews have a saying. 'Men should be careful about making women cry because God counts their tears.'"

"Perhaps God paid Landis a visit," Hazel said, shifting her flower basket.

"Anyone else making noise?"

"Just Clare. All I'm trying to do is keep my

husband's affairs quiet so my children's futures will not be harmed, and they will not hate him more than they do. As for this business of the hatchet, I couldn't tell you anything about it. Monahan didn't give me a name either when he told me about the tip."

"Speaking of children, why wasn't your daughter at the funeral?"

"She's attending school in Massachusetts. It would have been an arduous journey for her. I told her to stay put."

"Did Landis have any gambling debts?"

"Not that I'm aware."

"Besides women, did he have any other vices?"

"You mean like drugs, gambling, horses? My husband's great joy in life was to take away other people's joy, and he usually did it through sex or his bully pulpit—the bench."

"I don't know how you stood it, Hazel. All these years."

"He was so handsome when he was young, and I was young, too, and foolish, just ripe for the pickin'. It wasn't obvious what Landis was at the time. He was fun and hopeful for the future, but my mother knew. She said, 'Don't fall in love with Landis Garrett. If you hitch your wagon to that man, you'll rue the day.' I should have listened, but maybe I'll have some peace now."

"Do you have any idea who might have done this to Landis?"

"Anyone is possible."

"It has to be someone near, someone who knows the layout of both our properties. Is there an employee who had a recent blowup with Landis?"

"Mother!"

Both women looked toward the house.

A young man with sandy brown hair emerged from the house.

Hazel said to Mona, "You've got to leave. I don't want my son to see us talking."

The young man looked about and saw the two women standing in the garden. Seeing Mona was with his mother, he hurried over. "Miss Mona, may I ask what you are doing here?"

"Hello, Ben. I walked over to ask if there was anything I could do for your mother."

"If we needed any help, we wouldn't ask you."

"Ben," Hazel pleaded. "Don't."

Mona said, "I see. Please believe me that Mooncrest Enterprises are just as eager for justice to be found for your father as you are."

"Ha. Likely story," Ben said, standing close to his mother. "By the way, we want our dog back."

"You mean the dog your father was beating in the middle of a public road? That dog? I bought it from your father, and I have a bill of sale to prove it."

"You stole our dog," Ben asserted.

"The court said otherwise. Your father lost the case as I had paid your father for the dog, the privilege of paying the dog's vet bills, and restoring him to health."

"He was a champion coon dog."

Mona could see Ben had inherited the worst traits of his father—stubborn and stupid. There was no reasoning with him, so she decided to ignore him. "Hazel, call if you need anything. I hope to see your family at the ball next month. It's to raise money for charity."

"As if we would set foot in your house," Ben sneered.

"Suit yourself," Mona replied. She nodded to Hazel and turned to leave.

"If I catch you on Garrett property again, I'll have you arrested for trespassing," Ben called after her.

Mona kept on walking, disappointed with her visit. Strolling through fields shimmering with waving bluegrass, she heard tractors in the distance, cutting hay. She came to the stile and decided to have it taken down. There was no point in making it easy for anyone from Garrett's side to climb over to her property.

Hazel had not really given any useful information, but Ben's behavior was predictable. He was afraid of the town finding out about his father's indiscretions, so all the hullabaloo happening at Mooncrest Farm would not be in his best interest. He would want things to die down. Mona marked Hazel and Ben off the list.

Maybe the younger son?

Mona would use the servants' grapevine when she got home and see what she could find out that way. Picking up her pace, Mona hurried to the back of the manor in hopes of grabbing an oatmeal cookie she had seen Monsieur Bisaillon making earlier. Some cookies and a nice cup of tea sounded wonderful before Farley picked her up. She rounded a grove of shade trees and entered the back of the garden when she saw someone sitting near the rose bushes.

The visitor heard Mona and turned, waving a scarf in greeting.

Mona stopped short, thinking she was seeing a mirage.

The visitor jumped up, ran over, and kissed a stunned Mona. "Mona, darling! Your servants told me that you had taken a walk this way. I've been waiting for ages. Mona, you look positively stunned. I told Robert to keep my visit quiet. I see the darling has. Are you surprised? Are you?"

"Hello, Alice," Mona mumbled. "You're right. Robert kept your visit a secret." She pulled Alice's arms away from around her waist. "To what do I owe the pleasure?"

Alice beamed when she announced, "To get married! Mona, dearest, I came here to get married, and I want you to be my maid of honor!"

16

Mona felt dizzy as Lady Alice prattled on. She reached over to a tree trunk to steady herself.

"Why, Mona! What's wrong? You look as white as a ghost."

Mona regained her composure and decided to act like the lady she was. She saw no use in weeping profusely or acting out in a dramatic scene with Alice. After all, she had thrown away her chance for love by being too distant with Lord Farley. It was her own fault she had lost him.

"I hope you and Robert will be very happy, Alice."

"Robert!" Lady Alice looked nonplussed. "I'm not marrying Robert. I'm engaged to Ogden Nithercott. Look at my engagement ring. It was his grandmother's. Even though it's old, it looks very up-to-date. Isn't it pretty?"

Mona looked at a stunning, marquise cut, Burmese ruby with surrounding diamonds. "The Professor?"

Alice grinned. "The very same."

"Still, why are you here?"

"Ogden and I don't have any family to speak of in England, and we wanted to be with family when we got married. So, we decided to follow Robert back. You are my family, Mona. I want you to be with me when I take my vows."

Mona choked back the tears. "Alice, I *am* very happy for you. I know Nithercott adores you. He'll make you a fine husband."

"Really?"

"Very."

"Are you glad we came?"

"Yes, Alice. You have no idea how glad."

"I wondered if we should come. You didn't answer my letters, Mona. Robert said you didn't answer his letters either. Why?"

"I'll tell you one day, my sweet, when you are an old married lady, and affairs of the heart are a thing of the past."

"Oh, I don't like the sound of that. No affairs of the heart? Might as well be dead then."

"Let's sit down here among the sweet smelling roses, and you tell me all about it."

"Robert was very helpful, and saved Bosworth Manor for me. Within two months, I was able to rent out all the farms and purchase a new tractor. Robert instituted a system in which the farmers borrow my equipment. There is a sign up sheet on the equipment barn door, and farmers put down what days they need the equipment. All they have to do is pay for the petrol to run the equipment and bring it back to the barn each night.

"This has freed them up from acquiring equipment loans, and they are able to put more money into renovating their farms. Plus, they give one day a month's labor to restore Bosworth Manor, which I take off their rent. It's too late in the year for crops, but next year I should see a profit, as will the tenants between next year's planting and sheep. If that happens, I'll be able to pay off some of my debts. Cross your fingers."

"Extraordinary," was all Mona could say.

"I couldn't have done it without Robert. He

seems to have a knack for the land. After he straightened out Bosworth Manor, Robert checked on his father. He had a stroke but he's doing better than expected."

"That's wonderful, Alice, but how did things come about with Nithercott?"

"He would come on the weekends supposedly to help Robert, but I think it was to see me. Of course, a lot of the time Robert was out tramping in some field, so Ogden helped with the estate's books and paperwork. He was very helpful . . . and funny . . . and sweet. I realized one day when he wasn't at Bosworth Manor that I missed him—really missed his droopy face. Know what I mean? That's when I knew I was finally over Robert and could move on with my life."

"I thought you said you would be the perfect wife for Robert when he becomes a duke."

"I still would be, but here's the funny thing about love. It doesn't care about breeding or titles. It reaches into the deepest regions of our hearts and pulls at something primal. If you had told me that I would be marrying a professor of languages with no title, I would have said you were mad. But here I am, and I'm so happy I could burst."

Lady Alice reached across and held Mona's hand. "I feel rather ashamed of those ridiculous things I said to you in June. Can you ever forgive me for being so pompous . . . so English?"

"Forgiven and forgotten, my dear. Now, let's talk about the wedding."

"We're going to have it at Robert's estate. Very simple. Then we will honeymoon in Florida. I understand there is a railway that goes all the way to Key West. From there we will take a boat to the Bahamas and then back home on an English passenger ship."

"But you must have an engagement party. I insist on giving you one."

"That would be lovely, but aren't you having some sort of issue with the law?"

Mona cupped her cheeks in dismay. "Oh, dear, I am supposed to go to the sheriff's office this afternoon. I hope I haven't missed my appointment."

"Robert is waiting for you in the parlor. He brought me over."

Mona said, "Sweetie, I must go."

"I'll come, too. You can drop me off at Robert's place on your way into town."

ABIGAIL KEAM

Mona rushed to gather her hat, purse, and gloves.

Samuel stood at the front door with them waiting for Mona.

"Lord Farley is waiting for both you and Lady Alice in his car, Miss."

Mona grabbed her things. "Were you eavesdropping again, Samuel?"

"I observed through the window you and the other miss coming toward the house."

"So it was peeping this time."

"I merely anticipated my employer's needs," Samuel deadpanned. "Besides, it wasn't really me who saw, but Jetta and Violet, who were peeking out the window."

Mona laughed. She had always complained there was no privacy at Moon Manor. No wonder Robert wanted to take her for a drive in order to speak with her. She thought ahead of the drive home alone with him.

She wondered what he was going to say.

Don't break my heart, Robert, now that you are free from Alice. Please don't break my heart.

17

"I tried to tell you, but you were always so busy," Farley said.

"It was a shock to see Alice sitting in my rose garden."

"She and Ogden have spent a great deal of money coming to Kentucky so you could be included in their wedding."

"I realize that, but they couldn't have picked a worse time. This murder is hanging over my head like Damocles' sword."

"Let's put our best foot forward. We both want Alice and Nithercott to be happy. Let's show them what America has to offer even in the midst of a depression."

"It will be odd calling the groom Ogden."

"Just call him Nithercott. I do."

"Was Alice's arrival to Kentucky all you wanted to say?"

"I want to have a serious talk with you, but not now. Let's get this murder rap off your plate first."

Somewhat deflated, Mona leaned back in the car seat. She rolled down the window and enjoyed the wind blowing on her face. Mona was not going to throw herself at the feet of this man or any man. She had too much pride. Mona wasn't sure if Farley was stalling for some reason, or she had misread his intentions. Either way, she was going to keep quiet until he declared himself to her—if he ever did.

"Here we are," Farley said, turning into the parking lot of the sheriff's office.

"Dexter is here," Mona said, watching her lawyer hurry down the building's steps toward their car.

Farley stopped, letting Dexter climb into the back seat. "It's over, folks."

"What do you mean?" Mona asked, turning around in her seat.

"First of all, there were no fingerprints on the hatchet. It had been wiped clean, and the blood on the hatchet was from a chicken," Dexter said smugly.

"And the hair?" Farley asked.

"It was human hair, all right, but anyone could have pulled hair from their own head and placed it in the blood." Dexter patted Mona on the shoulder. "You don't have to give your fingerprints. I left Monahan feeling downright in the dumps."

"That's a relief," Mona said, smiling brightly.

"I told Monahan this was the end of the harassment. If he attempts to coerce you in the future, Mooncrest Enterprises will sue his department. He has found nothing that can tie you or anyone working at Mooncrest Farm to Landis Garrett's death."

"This is such happy news," Mona said. She felt a great burden lift from her shoulders.

"And that's not all," Dexter said, pulling a piece of paper from his briefcase and handing it to Mona. "I got a copy of the autopsy report. Garrett might not have been murdered at all."

Farley leaned over to read the report with Mona. "How did you get this?"

Dexter waved his hand in a dismissive manner. "Doesn't matter. Let's just say I have friends."

Mona looked up in astonishment. "It says Garrett died by drowning."

"Is that funny? Decapitation was postmortem," Dexter said, pointing to a comment on the autopsy report. "Any good lawyer can make the case that Landis Garrett drowned accidentally. Someone came along and found the body."

"And decided to decapitate him?" Farley asked, incredulously. "That's farfetched, don't you think, old boy?"

Both Mona and Dexter said in unison, "NO!"

"The most Sheriff Monahan can charge anyone with at this point is abuse of a corpse."

Mona shuddered. "Gruesome."

Farley asked, "You're saying there is no reason to believe murder even occurred?"

"Yes. I'm saying there is no proof a murder happened."

Mona pointed to the coroner's remarks. "Says the causes of bruises and cuts could not be determined."

Dexter said, "The river is high for this time of

the year and is full of debris. Garrett could have been tossed and battered by the current."

"I didn't know bodies could receive bruises after death," Farley said.

"This report doesn't say Garrett wasn't murdered. Just says he drowned," Mona commented.

Dexter groaned, "Please don't go looking for trouble, Mona. Accept this good luck and move on."

"We still need to find out who cut off Garrett's head and planted it on my property, Dexter. Someone is definitely going to a lot of trouble trying to implicate me in this mess."

"She's righto, old boy."

"You stay out of this, Farley," Dexter snapped. "And quit calling me 'old boy.'"

Farley didn't reply, but took out a cigarette from his case and lit it.

Mona waved the smoke away from her face, trying to hide her surprise at Dexter's retort to Farley. "Where do we go from here?"

"We'll keep investigating from our end, and you go on with your life. I'll handle things."

"May we proceed with the ball?"

"Go ahead," Dexter assured. "Send out the

invitations. As far as I'm concerned, this matter is over except for tying up a loose end or two."

"Then I'm going to have the ball in honor of Lady Alice. It can be an engagement party for her as well as a charity event."

"Lady Alice is here?"

Mona answered, "Yes, she's getting married."

Dexter gave Farley a sour look. "To you?"

Farley replied, "She's marrying a friend of mine."

"And Lady Alice came all the way to Kentucky to tie the knot?"

"She wanted me to be in the wedding," Mona said.

"Willie will like that I'm sure. Look, I've got to get back to the office." Dexter snatched the autopsy report out of Mona's hand and put it back in his briefcase.

"Thank you, Dexter. You have no idea how happy this makes me."

Dexter got out of the car and leaned in Mona's window. "I'll call off the Pinkertons. I think the worst is over."

Mona blew Dexter a kiss, not knowing a gathering storm was brewing her way.

18

The next few weeks were idyllic for Mona. Deciding not to wait, Lady Alice and her fiancé, Ogden Nithercott, pushed forward the date for their wedding. It was to be a small affair, so not much planning was needed for the blessed event.

Meanwhile, having free time on their hands, the couple gave talks to local organizations about their adventure in June describing in lurid detail Lady Alice's kidnapping and the discovery of Alexander the Great's signet ring. They became the toast of the town, so of course, everyone wanted to come to their wedding, which was being held at Lord Farley's home.

Not wanting hoards of strangers on his farm, Farley asked for a compromise. To satisfy the townspeople, Mona was to sponsor a public

wedding reception during her charity ball, which
Lady Alice and Nithercott agreed to attend.

The days rushed by quickly until the appoint-
ed day for the wedding arrived. It was a beautiful
day for nuptials. The colorful trees were at the
height of their glory, and the sky was brilliant
bright cobalt with cumulus clouds lazily drifting
over.

The Deatherages were invited, as were the
mayor and his wife along with some professors
from University of Kentucky whom Nithercott
had met. Violet and Jetta also came.

Lady Alice wore a long-sleeved, antique white,
satin dress with an elongated sheer veil. She was
beautiful, and Nithercott was almost handsome in
his tux. Alice regally took her place beside
Nithercott as they stood before the minister.

Nithercott beamed at Alice with such love,
Mona wondered if his shoes would keep his feet
to the floor or would he float upward from sheer
happiness. His demeanor caused Mona to think
of her own future and happiness.

Mona took Alice's bouquet and proudly stood
in as maid of honor while Farley was Nithercott's
best man. During the ceremony, Mona glanced

over and saw Farley staring at her. She quickly looked away. They had never had their talk, and Mona wasn't going to push the issue. It had been so hectic, she and Farley hadn't found time to be alone together. They would find the time to sit down and say the things that mattered to each other after the ball. Perhaps.

After the wedding, there was a small cake along with tea sandwiches and finger food provided by Bisaillon on the sideboard in Farley's dining room.

Jetta had to talk a stubborn Monsieur Bisaillon into making the wedding cake and food for the private reception. At first, he refused Mona's request to provide the reception's repast. "I have too much to do as it is now. Let Lord Farley's cook prepare the wedding luncheon!" he shouted.

However, Jetta said pictures were to be taken for the newspaper. Well, that was a slice of a different cake. Once on board, Bisaillon pulled out his pastry cookbooks and made a white cake with buttercream icing decorated with sugar magnolias. He then planned a stupendous wedding cake for the charity ball which he called his "masterpiece." No one was allowed to see his recipe or decoration design, which was locked away in Bisaillon's desk. Obbie and Jed were sworn to secrecy, and even tempting bribes from Thomas would not unlock their lips. Everyone would have to wait and see.

After the reception, Alice dressed in a soft pearl gray suit. Coming down the staircase, she threw her wedding bouquet of white gardenias.

Blushing, Violet caught it. Jetta looked at her with envy, which was not lost on Mona.

According to social mores, Mona and Jetta were spinsters, but that was not their problem. Loneliness was the problem.

While Mona could live a single life and have no regrets, she doubted Jetta would be happy not having a husband and a family. Mona always found the best thing for her to do when feeling down was to work or help someone else. Perhaps she should do a little matchmaking for Jetta. It would take her own mind off Farley.

After saying quick goodbyes, Mr. and Mrs. Ogden Nithercott left to spend the night at the Phoenix Hotel before leaving for a quick honeymoon. The Deatherages and the professors had a quick drink and left. The mayor had another piece of cake until his wife complained her bridge group was waiting on her.

Jetta and Violet began cleaning up when Farley said his staff would tend to the mess. They were guests and not expected to help. Violet twittered "thank you" like an excited bird while Jetta merely nodded. She was ready to go back to Moon Manor and have a hot bath to soothe her nerves. They left together by the back door and headed across the fields.

Mona gathered her purse and gloves. "I'd better go, too."

Farley reached for her hand.

Mona gladly placed her small hand in his meaty one.

"Must you go?" he asked.

Mona shook her head. "No, I don't have to go."

Farley pulled Mona to him and wrapped his arms around her, laying his cheek against hers. "Tell me you thought about me while I was gone."

She confessed, "I did. Every day. Every time a whippoorwill cried, I thought of you."

"Don't mock me. Why didn't you write,

Mona? I waited every day for a letter."

"It's hard to explain, but I wanted you to be sure about Alice—about me. I didn't want to influence you in any way. If you were going to forget about me, then this was the time to do so because it would have been a clean break."

"Clean? It was torture."

"And there is . . . your penchant for women."

"I've lived a man's life. I make no apologies about it."

"Men who live such lives leave a trail of broken lives behind them."

Farley grabbed Mona by the shoulders. "Hey, of what are you accusing me?"

"When I give my heart to someone, I want him to be a man of honor—not some playboy."

He pushed her away. "I risked my neck for you. I've never lied to you about anything. I'm not a saint, but if that's what you want, there's the door."

Mona's face flushed with anger. "Now wait a minute. If you think I'm going to fall into your arms because you crook your little finger, you're barking up the wrong tree, mister."

"Stupid analogy, but then you're a stupid

American cow."

Mona gasped. "Stupid? Well, isn't that the pot calling the kettle black?"

"Stupid and funny looking with all that white hair and yellow eyes. You look like something out of a horror film. And you take yourself way too seriously."

"Yeah?" Mona yelled.

"Yeah."

"How many times have I told you not to call me a cow?" Mona picked up a glass and threw it at Farley.

He ducked. "And you throw like a girl."

Mona picked up a dessert plate and threw it at Farley. It crashed against the wall.

Farley laughed. "LIKE A GIRL!"

"Ooh, you make me so mad," Mona said, stomping her foot. She picked up a wine glass and threw it at him.

"Quit breaking my glassware. That's crystal you know."

"Only a 'girl' would be concerned about the crystal. Be glad I'm not throwing knives." She picked up another wine glass.

"That's it," Farley said. He rushed Mona,

swept her up in his arms, and ran to the pool where he dumped her in the deep end.

Mona bobbed up, coughing. "Oh, my beautiful dress. It's ruined. It was chiffon."

Farley mocked her using a falsetto voice. "Only a 'girl' would be concerned about her chiffon."

Mona pursed her lips in defiance and, reaching up, grabbed a hold of Farley's legs and pulled him into the pool.

Farley came up sputtering water. "You little devil," he said, giving Mona an evil look.

Mona squealed and swam toward the shallow end.

Farley pulled her back, but Mona kicked him. "Ouch."

"Serves you right."

Farley swam after Mona, catching up with her in the shallow area. Grabbing Mona, he pulled her close. "Stop fighting me, Mona. Quit squirming." He shook her. "Stop it, I say."

Mona became still and looked up at Farley. "What do you want from me, Robert?"

"Everything. Your body. Your heart. If I could eat your soul, I would. I want to devour you, Mona, and leave nothing for the crows." He kissed Mona as though his life depended on it. He conveyed everything in that kiss—his deep love for Mona, his dreams for their future, and his regrets about the past.

As though telepathic, Mona knew what Farley was trying to express. It was as if she could read his mind.

They stayed in the pool for a long time before returning to Farley's house.

Mona didn't make it back home until the wee hours of the morning.

19

Mona was wearing Farley's shirt and a pair of his trousers when she made her way to the back entrance of Moon Manor. It was then she realized she didn't have the key to the back door. The key in her purse was for the front door only. Luckily she had the purse tucked in her waistband. She was proceeding to the front of the mansion when she spied a light flashing in a grove of trees to the left of the house. It was after three in the morning. Who would be out this late at night but lovers and malcontents?

She took the gun out of her purse and followed the light. She could see a figure skulking from tree to tree ahead, and she crept quietly, allowing the moving light ahead to guide her way until it stopped. Mona hunkered down, knowing the prowler had come to the limestone rock fence that defined the property line between Mooncrest Farm and the Garrett's property.

The light swished this way and that. Mona deduced the prowler was probably looking for the stile she had removed. Seeing none, he bounded over the fence.

Mona deduced the night stalker had to be a young male by the way she saw the black clad figure climb over the fence. That was no easy task in the dark, even with a flashlight.

Mona followed, but had a much harder time climbing over the fence. She scraped her hands and elbows, pulling herself up and over. Once she stepped on a twig, making a snapping noise and causing her to jump behind a Rose of Sharon bush.

The prowler stopped, turned off the flashlight, and lay flat on the ground.

Mona knew he was surveying the grounds, looking for anything suspicious. She waited patiently, trying not to move.

A fox moseyed past looking for juicy insects and rodents. Alarmed at encountering Mona, she yipped.

Please don't bite me and give me rabies, Mona silently pleaded.

Without so much as a by-your-leave, the fox dismissed Mona as no threat and went about her way searching for edibles.

The prowler must have seen the fox as well and believed it responsible for the noise. He got up and continued to the patio at the back of the Garrett house. Turning off the flashlight, he took out a knife and stealthily pried open the kitchen screen door.

Mona didn't know what to do. Should she raise the alarm for the Garretts, or should she watch and wait to see what the prowler would do? She chose the latter. Sneaking closer, she watched the man enter and disappear into the darkness of the Garrett's house. She couldn't make out where the intruder had gone in the house. Believing she couldn't let a possibly dangerous man harm those asleep, Mona moved to call out but suddenly saw the flashlight beam in Landis' office. Deciding to take a chance, she moved closer to the house and peered in the window. She could see the intruder search Landis' desk first and then behind paintings and through books.

A lamp turned on in an upstairs bedroom, which flooded the patio area with light.

Still holding the gun in her hand, Mona shrank against the house and tried to meld into the shadows.

The intruder saw the light fall upon the patio. He silently opened the office's French doors leading to the patio and rushed across the lawn.

As a shot was fired from an upstairs window, the intruder briefly glanced back at the house, giving Mona a good look at his face.

It was her new farm manager, Kenesaw Mountain!

Another shot pierced the night.

Hearing Hazel screaming, Mona realized she had to get out of there! Running in the opposite direction of Kenesaw, she headed toward where the plank fences began on her property. Finding the wooden fence line, she climbed over them quickly and hurried back to Moon Manor. Mona slowed down only when she reached the garden area to put the gun back in her purse. She was grateful Moon Mansion was still dark. No one had heard the gunshots, and obviously, the Garretts hadn't called the house.

She ran around to the front of the manor and let herself in. Hurrying upstairs she unlocked the door to the master suite, confident Violet was sound asleep and blissfully snoring.

Mona threw off Farley's clothes and climbed into bed where Chloe waited wagging her tail. She pulled the dog close and whispered, "Chloe, I found out a secret tonight. Kenesaw Mountain is a risk taker just like me."

20

"Are you sure it was Kenesaw Mountain?" Farley asked.

Mona poured them both a cup of coffee. "I'm positive."

"After all, it was dark, and you were exhausted," Farley said, winking.

"I don't like being second-guessed, especially by men. I find it an irritating trait," Mona groused.

"Oh, I believe you. Just teasing."

"You forget that I don't like being teased. I think it's a cruel sport."

"What do you intend to do? Call Dexter?"

"No. Dexter is the one who hired Kenesaw. I think I need someone objective to look into this for me."

"I know a private dick."

"That's something you should keep to yourself."

"Look who's teasing now. Pass the cream, will ya?"

"Do you really know someone who might help?"

"Yeah, but he's a dog."

"Don't insult Chloe's kind."

"What I mean to say is that he'll do anything for money."

"What's his name?"

"He goes by the name of Jellybean Martin."

"How do you know him?"

"I've hired him for a couple of jobs."

Mona's eyes narrowed. "What kind of jobs?"

"You never mind. You don't need to go through my past as I won't go through yours."

"Agreed."

"We move forward."

"Aye, aye, sir," Mona replied.

"Speaking of moving forward, you took a big chance following that mug last night. You could have been killed. What were you thinking?"

"I was thinking I could catch the person who

was trying to frame me."

"And if you caught him, what did you intend to do."

"I had my gun. I intended to turn him over to the authorities."

"You were willing to shoot him? Because that's what you would have had to do. You would have been alone with a dangerous nutcase in the middle of the night. He could have easily jumped you and turned the gun on you. If he just ran away, were you willing to shoot him in the back? You put yourself in an impossible situation."

"I hate it when you're right."

Farley bit into a piece of toast and said with his mouth full, "I'm always right."

"No, Farley. I'm always right."

"I liked it better when you called me Robert. Now we're back to Farley."

"I can always call you Lord Bob."

"I hate that. What happened to Robert? You called me Robert last night."

Mona looked about. "Shush. You know how my staff eavesdrops. They don't need to know about us."

"Why not?"

"Because I need to get used to the idea myself."

"Are you having second thoughts?"

"What I need is to have you quit harping on what I call you and help me think what to do."

Farley offered, "Let me phone this Jellybean chap."

"Can I meet him at your house? I don't want anyone to know I'm hiring him."

"Okay by me."

"That means you will have to send your staff away while we meet."

"I'll find some errand for them to run."

"Good. When can you arrange it?"

"How about this evening?"

"I can say that I'm coming over to swim."

"Sounds pretty good to me. Are you going to go au naturel like you did last night?"

"I'll be wearing a proper bathing suit as you will."

"Darn. What would people say if they knew what a sybarite you really are, Miss Madeline Mona Moon?"

"I'm sure they would not be surprised. The only thing I haven't been accused of so far is cannibalism."

"Give them time."

Violet stuck her head out the patio door. "Miss Mona, Mr. Mountain is here to see you."

Mona and Farley looked at each other.

"Speak of the devil," Farley said, chuckling.

"Send him out, Violet. Thank you," Mona said, pinching Farley under the table.

Kenesaw walked out holding a clipboard and wearing a white shirt with khaki pants. "Sorry to interrupt your breakfast, folks."

"Please join us," Mona said.

"Already had my breakfast, but thanks." Kenesaw sat easily in a chair. "I have the job roster for this week. I was wondering if you would look it over and approve it."

"Managing the farm is your job, Kenesaw," Mona replied, looking over the roster.

"I know, but I want to hire two more men to help clean out the south pasture over on Bowman Mill Road. That's where we're going to put some of the broodmares and their foals."

"Do we have adequate shelter for them?"

"We are building a shed for them now."

"And they have plenty of water?"

"A stream runs right through the meadow."

"Go ahead for now, but I'll want to check it later this month."

"Good. I'll go ahead and hire two more men today."

"Two less men out of a job," Farley said, rising from the table.

Mona caught Kenesaw giving Farley a sharp look. Kenesaw's jovial countenance dropped for only a second, but Mona knew Kenesaw didn't like Farley. What other secrets was Kenesaw trying to hide?

"So where will you be today, Kenesaw?" Mona asked.

"I'll be in town looking for workers, and then I'll go straight to Bowman Mill Road. Do you need me for something?"

"Just like to keep tabs on my employees from time to time."

Farley pulled Mona out of her seat. "I need to stretch my legs. Go for a walk with me."

"A short one. Then I've got to get to my office. Jetta will be waiting for me." She turned to Kenesaw. "That will be all, Kenesaw. Thank you."

Mona took Farley's arm as they strolled toward the river. Glancing back, she saw Kenesaw staring after them, scowling.

Seeing Mona look back, Kenesaw's face brightened into a smile as he waved.

Mona was dismayed. Why hadn't she sensed the seething rage beneath the beguiling smile of Kenesaw Mountain? What was he hiding?

21

The door to Kenesaw's white framed cottage on the Mooncrest Farm was unlocked. Mona and Farley entered and stood in the threshold looking about. The cottage was tidy but sparse. There was a couch and a couple of chairs near the fireplace and a new Crosley radio held court near the front window. All the curtains were closed, making the room feel small and drab.

Farley remarked, "This place needs a new coat of paint."

"It's stuffy, too," Mona added. "Kenesaw obviously never opens a window."

"Shall we?"

"Let's get this over with." Mona stepped inside. "You take the bedroom and bath. I'll take the kitchen and this room."

"You won't have to look behind any paintings as there are none. Not even a girly calendar hanging on the wall," Farley said as he strode into the bedroom.

Mona stood in the middle of the living room and looked about. Where to start? She went over to the fireplace and stuck her arm up the chimney looking for anything. Nothing but soot. Her arm was dirty, so she went into the kitchen to wash. After cleaning herself up, Mona went through the cabinets, looked under the kitchen table and chairs, poked around the small freezer in the refrigerator, searched through his flour and sugar tins, even pulled his small stove out and checked behind it. Nothing. She went back into the living room when Farley came out from the bathroom.

He shook his head.

Together they searched the couch and the two chairs and came up zero.

Mona plopped into one of the chairs. "This certainly is frustrating."

"Are you sure he took something from the Garrett's house?"

"I saw him tuck a file and other papers into his waistband. Kenesaw left with them all right."

"Perhaps, he dropped them as he ran from the house?"

"Possibly, but let's keep going."

Farley looked around. "What do you suggest?"

Mona sighed until she glanced at the big Crosley. It was a floor model, about four feet tall. "Can you open the back of the radio?"

"I'll see if there is a screwdriver in the kitchen." Farley went into the kitchen, rattled through some drawers, and came back with a screwdriver. "Voila!"

Mona clapped her hands.

Farley scooted the radio away from the window and opened the back. "Golly, as I live and breathe." He took several files out and handed them to Mona. "They were laid up right against some tubes. It's a wonder they didn't start a fire."

Mona motioned for Farley to sit next to her. Handing him one of the files, she said, "Here. Go through this."

"Let's just take them."

"Then Kenesaw will know that we are on to him. Just go through the files."

Farley snapped to attention and saluted. "Yes,

Captain." He sat down and went through a sheaf of papers. "This contains financial records and bank statements for the Garrett family."

"Who in the family?"

"Mostly the old man, but his sons as well." Farley studied one of the statements. "Bloody hell, Landis was loaded."

"Let me see." Studying the statement, Mona quickly scanned the figures. "I don't think a judge makes this kind of money. There's over forty thousand dollars in this one account alone."

"Landis had accounts in multiple banks. Look, this account is in a bank in Louisville and this one is in Cincinnati."

"I think a good accountant could go through these statements and prove Landis was as dirty as they come."

"Perhaps Kenesaw is gathering evidence to turn over to the authorities. He might be acting undercover."

"Anything is possible, I guess."

Farley asked, "What's in your file?"

"It's a list of names and initials listed under the heading of the Pegasus Association," Mona said. She pointed to the letterhead which consisted of the name under the logo of the winged Pegasus. "The address is a post office box."

"Let me see the list." Farley perused the names. "There are some big hitters here. There's a MM on this list. Could mean Melanie Moon?"

"We know half a dozen people with the initials MM. Could be anyone."

"The initials might mean those members are silent partners. It seems odd that there are no addresses or phone numbers. Just a list of ten names and initials. Have you heard of this group?"

Farley shook his head. "No, but all these names are connected one way or another to horse racing. See this name here? He's connected with the criminal underworld, and his name had been bandied about in reference to the death of Phar Lap."

"Who's Phar Lap?"

"Really, Mona. You should brush up on the Thoroughbred racing world since you own a horse farm. He was one of the greatest racehorses of all times and died last year under suspicious circumstances in California. Some say by arsenic poisoning."

"I see two of our friends on this list. Would they be consorting with a known criminal?"

"Sometimes a person doesn't have a choice. These men reach out and what are you going to do—say no and wind up having your head cut off and placed in a bucket? Maybe that's what happened to Landis?"

"Landis Garrett's name is not on this list."

"Perhaps he said no."

"Let's put this stuff back and get out of here."

Farley put the files back and screwed the panel back on the radio.

Peering out the front window, Mona made sure no one was around before she and Farley left the cottage. They parted at the back of the garden with Farley going to his house and Mona hurrying to her office before Jetta came looking for her.

Hopefully, Farley's man, Jellybean, would have some answers for her later.

Mona was counting on him.

22

Mona walked through Farley's patio door, wearing beach pajama pants, crop top, and a floppy hat. She found Farley speaking with a small, middle-aged man in the receiving parlor. The little man was black, wore a Fedora hat sporting a peacock feather, a dark, finely-tailored suit, and polished Florsheim wingtip shoes. He seemed quite at ease sitting in a dainty chintz-covered chair in the parlor, drinking a cold beer from a chilled mug.

Farley smiled and beckoned to Mona, saying, "Miss Mona Moon, this is Jellybean Martin. Mr. Martin, this is your client, Miss Moon."

Jellybean stood up and doffed his hat. "Miss, glad to metcha." He reached out to shake Mona's hand.

Mona shook his hand heartily. "Likewise, Mr. Martin."

"Ah, call me Jellybean."

"That's a very unusual moniker. May I inquire as to the origin of your name?"

"When I was young, I loved ragtime music, so folks started calling me Jellybean after Jelly Roll Morton. That cat could really tickle the ivories."

"Not Jelly Roll?"

Martin grinned, "Well, I'm also partial to jelly beans. The red ones especially. Never without them." He pulled a ragged paper bag from his pants pocket. "See."

Mona laughed and sat across from Jellybean. "Yes."

Jellybean took another sip from his beer. "Excuse me for drinking in front of you, but I haven't had any lunch. Lord Farley told me this was urgent."

"I can make you a sandwich, Jellybean," Farley offered.

"No, thank you. This is fine."

"May I ask how you obtain your information?"

"You ask that because I'm black?"

"Frankly, yes. Many of the usual ways to investigate are unavailable to you, I'm sorry to say."

"No need to apologize, Miss. The world is what it is, but I need you to understand I'm not an official private detective. I don't have a license. What I provide is information. I hang around pool halls, bars, and whorehouses, Miss. You'd be surprised what a fella' can learn when men get drunk and their lips loosen. I also have contacts with most of the black employees in all the houses, great and small. I know just about everything that goes on in this town. Pardon my boasting." Jellybean took another sip of beer and downed a handful of jelly beans.

"Doesn't the peacock feather gain some unwanted attention?" Mona asked.

"Most folks are used to seein' me hang around. They pay me no mind."

"I see. Well, Lord Farley told you my problem. Have you any information for me?"

"Miss Moon, you are in danger."

"What!" Mona gasped.

"I ain't gonna mince words with a lady such as yourself. You know about the Pegasus Association?"

"I saw that heading on a letter with a list of names and initials.

"The Pegasus Association is a group of powerful men vying with the Kentucky Association for a new racetrack in the Bluegrass. A lot of money is involved."

"Why should that concern me? I have nothing to do with building racetracks. In fact, Mooncrest Farm doesn't even race anymore. We are now a breeding and boarding facility."

Farley intervened, "Why fight over a racetrack? No one has any money to gamble on horses. Most people are too broke."

Jellybean said, "These men are looking to the future when the Depression is over, Lord Farley. Sure, times are hard now, but things will pick up one day. This is all about the future."

"Does this group have anything to do with Landis Garrett's death?" Mona asked.

"Word on the street was he was feeding information to both groups. He wanted to be on the winning team, regardless of the coin flipping heads or tails."

"That certainly will get a person killed," Farley muttered.

"How did you come by seeing this list? The identity of the members is a closely guarded secret."

Farley said, "We found the documents from the back of a Crosley radio, which belongs to Kenesaw Mountain, Miss Moon's farm manager."

"Do you know how he got that information?"

"He stole it from Landis Garrett's house," Farley answered.

"Hmm, God bless him," Jellybean muttered. "I need to think on this. What is this Kenesaw's intent?"

Mona asked, "Is there anything else I need to know?"

"That's all I have on such short notice, but I'll nosey around. Put out some feelers and see what I pick up." He looked at his pocket watch. "I'd best be getting back to town."

"I didn't see a car outside."

Farley grinned. "To keep this meeting a secret, I met Jellybean in a graveyard."

"Yeah, I jumped in the back of Lord Farley's car, and he threw a blanket over me. I can't afford for folks to see me with him, and it's too dangerous to meet in town."

"Is all the cloak and dagger really necessary? We are beginning to sound like a Dorothy L. Sayers mystery," Mona complained.

"It's what I live for," Farley said.

Mona said, "I know you think this is fun, but it has me worried."

Jellybean said, "You best listen to the English gent, miss. These swells play for keeps."

"I must take my charge back into town. You go for a swim and then head to Moon Manor. I'll be back later, and you can berate me for my faults then," Farley said. "Chin chin."

Jellybean stood to leave.

When Mona stood, she noticed the diminutive gentleman came only to her shoulders. Although short and slight of build, Jellybean was wiry and hadn't an ounce of fat on him. Mona had no doubt he could take care of himself when push came to shove. "Thank you, again."

"I'll be in touch," Jellybean said.

Farley ushered him out to the back where his car waited.

Mona followed them out, watching Jellybean get in the back of the car, and Farley throw a blanket over him.

The charade made her uneasy.

Perhaps Mona should consider taking her cut of the Moon fortune and walk away. She didn't need all this drama in her life. It was a very tempting thought, and something Mona was going to consider.

Maybe throwing in the towel was the right thing to do.

23

The next several weeks were calm and peaceful. Mona, Jetta, and Violet concentrated on the charity ball. Even Willie pitched in, albeit in a supervisory capacity. Willie loved giving orders.

Excitement reached a new level when Babe Ruth confirmed he would be at the event. He was coming in the day before on the same train as Lady Alice and Nithercott, who were returning from their honeymoon.

Mona prayed the train would not be delayed causing the guests of honor to be absent. Without them, the charity event would be a dud. The invitations had been mailed, and ninety percent on the guest list had accepted.

Everything was going splendidly until Farley dropped by Moon Manor one evening.

Mona knew from his expression something was wrong.

"Can you take a break?"

"Sure. Jetta, can you finish with the florist?"

"Assuredly," Jetta replied, studying Farley's behavior. Not wanting to draw attention to him, Jetta continued discussing the buffet centerpiece with the florist. It had been decided to have all white flowers, and the florist was not sure the order could be filled so late in the fall.

Mona excused herself and followed Farley outside to the garden and beyond to the horse pastures. He stopped at a fence and looked about.

Seeing Mona and Farley, several mares wandered over, thinking they might get a treat. Mona stroked the muzzle of one of them. "What's wrong?"

"Jellybean is dead."

"What!" Mona exclaimed.

"My maid just told me. He was found early this morning in an alley with his throat cut. It will be in the evening paper."

"Oh, that poor fellow. Do you think his death has anything to do with us?"

"He called last night, saying he had information. Wanted to see me. I had made arrangements to pick him up late tonight."

"Does he have any family? Is there anything we can do?"

"Let me see what else I can find out."

"I wonder what information Jellybean had for us? I'm dreadfully upset over this. I liked him very much."

"So did I. Jellybean was a good egg."

Mona asked, "Shall we go to the police?"

"It happened within the city limits where Sheriff Monahan has no jurisdiction, but I still would stay as far away from the city police as I can. Let's see if they come to us."

"Did Jellybean say what it was about?"

"Just said he had found something, which might shed light on why Garrett died. Regardless, you better have an alibi ready for last night and this morning."

"I can vouch for my whereabouts. What about you?"

"Played poker with the boys last night. My staff can swear I was home most of the day. I'll be okay." Farley leaned over and kissed Mona.

"How's my favorite girl?"

"Frantic. We've less than two days to get this ball on track, and we are woefully behind."

"Anything I can do?"

"Stay out of the way."

"I was hoping you would say that. Heard anything from the Garretts?"

"Nothing, except that they are coming to the ball."

Farley pulled a wisp of platinum hair out of Mona's eyes. "I haven't read anything about their robbery in the paper."

"I don't think they reported it."

"What about Kenesaw?"

"I've had him working on other farms, but he'll be at the ball. He's in charge of taking care of Babe Ruth."

"I would have thought you'd have Dexter take charge with Ruth."

"I want to keep Kenesaw occupied."

"Have you talked to Dexter about Kenesaw yet?"

"I was hoping to have more information from Jellybean before I broached the subject with Dexter. Right now all I have is supposition. I need facts."

"I'll talk to my maid to see what else she may know, but I doubt I'll get anything out of her. She's pretty upset."

"I will talk to Thomas as well. He seems well informed about the goings on in town."

"Let's not lose heart over this, Mona," Farley said as he hugged Mona. One of the mares chewed the sleeve of his jacket. "Don't you feed these horses?"

"Shoo. Shoo. Stop that," Mona ordered, pushing the horse's head away.

"I've got to go. Keep me informed if you learn anything."

"I will," Mona promised. She watched Farley jump the fence into the pasture and walk toward his home. The mares followed him at a discreet distance, occasionally swishing their tails.

Mona looked back at the Moon Mansion, which was bustling with activity, people hurrying to and fro, vehicles jamming the driveway, burgoo simmering in large cauldrons, and workers putting up chairs and tables.

Mona hoped for everyone's sake that nothing would go wrong, but she felt the noose getting tighter and tighter around her neck.

24

The day before the charity ball finally arrived, and Mona sighed with relief.

Babe Ruth was ensconced upstairs with a diluted bottle of bourbon while Alice and Ogden occupied a large suite at the other end of the house. All three had come in on the same train but were taken to Moon Manor in separate cars.

Ruth was disappointed that a large crowd hadn't met him at the train station, but Dexter explained he had lied about the time Ruth was to arrive so as not to tire him out before the big day. Actually, it was to protect Moon Enterprises because Dexter was afraid a reporter would whisk Ruth off, and no one would see either one of them until an *exclusive* hit the papers while *the Bambino* lay drunk in some seedy hotel. Ruth seemed okay with the explanation, and Dexter rewarded him with a splendid dinner and unlimited glasses of champagne at Moon Manor, of course.

Alice and Nithercott pretended to be interested in Ruth's stories about baseball, but they had no idea who Ty Cobb or Shoeless Jackson was. Around ten, they pleaded exhaustion from their trip and fled to their suite. However, Dexter was enthralled with Ruth, and they sat up swapping stories and drinking in the library.

Mona and Jetta both said their goodnights and went to their respective rooms.

Violet and Chloe were waiting in Mona's suite. A fire in the fireplace threw shadows upon the walls as the wind picked up outside. Violet closed the doors to the suite's balcony. "It's starting to get cold. Winter's on the way."

"It needs to be sunny and the low sixties tomorrow. I'll be thrilled if the weather cooperates," Mona mused.

"Did you have a nice dinner with Mr. Ruth?"

Mona stepped out of her velvet gown. "Mr. Ruth has such a strong personality, he sucks up all the air in the room, but I like him. Ruth seems a compassionate person. He sure lives life to the fullest."

Violet picked up the dress and hung it up in the dressing room. "Thomas is serving drinks in the library, listening to his stories. He's thrilled for him to be here."

"It was a great idea of his to ask Ruth to come. It seems our Mr. Thomas played a little baseball in his youth. Was a pitcher, so he said. When I left he and Ruth were trading statistics. I'm going to make sure Ruth signs a baseball for Thomas." Mona wiped off her lipstick. "Violet, what was the last count of people coming tomorrow?"

"Two thousand."

"Can you imagine?"

"Mr. Mountain thinks we might have as many as five thousand people come to see Mr. Ruth."

Mona calculated in her head. "Five thousand people at twenty-five cents is over twelve hundred dollars. That's a lot of money to give to charity, but I hope we don't have so many. We can't accommodate five thousand people. We don't have the resources." She sat down and took off her stockings.

"Monsieur Bisaillon has spent days making five hundred caramel apples plus the League of Women Voters are bringing four carloads of homemade cakes and pies to sell. Jetta also bought a thousand Baby Ruth candy bars, and we have enough burgoo to serve over a thousand people. There also will be hard cider, Coca-Cola, and iced tea."

"What about water?"

"We will have water stations throughout the farm."

"Did you buy those new paper cups for water like I requested? I don't want glass broken all over the property."

"Well, Coca-Cola is a sponsor, and they delivered their drink in glass bottles, but they would be hard to break. They are going to have ice delivered first thing tomorrow to chill the bottles. As for the other drinks, we told people to bring their own containers. It's written on their tickets, but we do have glassware in case they forget."

Mona frowned.

Violet was quick to add. "Jetta did order paper cups for water."

"That's good, but what if you run out of

glasses for the other drinks?"

"We have a crew to pick up the glasses and wash them to reuse."

"Make sure some kind of disinfectant is used in the wash water."

"Obbie and Jed are in charge of the glass-ware."

"Good. I feel better now. Make sure they have time to enjoy the afternoon event."

"They're going to take turns."

"Okay. It seems like you and Jetta have every-thing under control for the afternoon event."

"Kenesaw said some of our workers were pulling together to cook hot dogs and hamburg-ers for folks. A dime for a hot dog and twenty cents for a hamburger," Violet replied, "but the money's not going to charity. The workers are going to keep the profits."

Mona went to her vanity and rubbed a night cream on her face. "I don't mind as long as they put a sign up saying where the money is going. I don't want our visitors to think we cheated them." She took a towel and wiped the cream off. "I hope we have enough staff to cover this affair. Thank goodness the afternoon event is only for three hours. We don't want to tire Mr. Ruth before the ball tomorrow night."

"Jetta has conscripted most of the Mooncrest workers with the promise of extra pay."

"Only seems fair."

"And their kids get to meet Mr. Ruth personally."

Mona chuckled. "Using their children to get close to Mr. Ruth. What a ruse. What else did *I* promise?"

"Free food for the workers."

"Which means I am subsidizing the hot dogs and hamburgers. Very clever."

"We didn't think you would mind."

"I don't. I have other things on my mind."

"Like the handsome Lord Farley?"

"Huh?" Mona seemed distracted. "Oh, Lord Farley. Yes. He's been on his best behavior since he's come back."

"Lady Alice seems happy with her new husband."

"Yes. They do seem suited to one another. I hope they will be very happy together."

Violet ventured, "Do you have marriage on your mind, Miss Mona?"

"If I do, Violet, you will be the first to know."

"Oh."

"Violet, it's going to be a long day tomorrow. Let's get some shut eye."

"Yes, Miss Mona."

"Don't forget to lock your bedroom door. With Mr. Ruth three sheets to the wind, you don't want him to stumble into your room by mistake."

Violet's eyes widened. "Goodness, no."

"Good night, Violet."

"Good night, Miss."

Violet shut the connecting door which led through the dressing room and bathroom to the maid's room.

Mona punched up her pillows and allowed Chloe under the covers. Soon Chloe was asleep, occasionally twitching. Mona wondered if Chloe was chasing a rabbit in her dreams. She envied Chloe's ability to sleep so soundly but doubted she would get much rest. The awful murder of Jellybean was on her mind. He would have opened a door with the information he had gathered. Now that door was shut. It was not lost on Mona as soon as a door was opened to some hint of truth, it shut soundly in her face. She couldn't get a lock on anything.

As soon as the ball was over and Mr. Ruth sent on his way, Mona would look into Jelly-bean's death. Somehow, his murder had to be tied up with Landis Garrett's death.

Mona just knew it.

25

When Mona rose the next morning, she was still exhausted. She had tossed and turned all night.

Chloe scratched at the door.

"You need to go potty?" Mona asked the poodle while unlocking her bedroom door.

Chloe shot out the door and down the staircase.

Mona smiled. She knew Chloe was heading toward the kitchen where Obbie would let her out to tinkle and then feed her.

Car horns and shouts floated up the stairs. Mona stood in the hallway listening. It was only seven, but the staff was already preparing for the day's events. The kitchen help had probably been up since four.

Mona quickly took a shower and dressed in a cotton shirt and pants. She wrapped a scarf around her hair and went down to the kitchen to see if she could help.

It was soon made clear to Mona by Monsieur Bisaillon that she was in the way. Getting the message her presence was not desired, Mona gathered Chloe, and they marched over to Lord Farley's abode.

"What are you doing here?" Farley asked, looking up from his newspaper in the breakfast nook.

"I was basically thrown out of my own home. Can I get some breakfast? There's nothing to eat but caramel apples at my house. I got caught sampling one, and Monsieur Bisaillon threw a fit."

"Sampling?"

"I wanted to make sure they were up to par."

"Of course."

"Please. Can I have something to eat? I'm famished."

Farley called to his housekeeper. "Can you fix Miss Mona breakfast? She is surely going to faint from hunger if we don't get some vittles down her gullet."

Mona made a face.

"And give something to that mangy dog of hers as well."

"You hurt Chloe's feelings when you say such things about her."

"You think Chloe understands what I say, Mona?"

"Of course, she does."

"Uh huh."

"Did you get any sleep last night?"

"No. You?"

Mona shook her head. "I kept thinking of poor Mr. Martin."

"Be careful today. Make sure Moon Manor is locked up tight this afternoon, and keep Violet with you at all times."

"Not possible. She has specific duties today."

"Then hang with Alice and Ogden."

"Where are you going to be?"

"I'm going to spend time with my poker buddies to see if I can pick up any useful information."

"Will you be at the afternoon event and charity ball?"

"I've paid for both in advance. Don't worry.

I'll be at your side during the ball."

Mona sighed. "Today was supposed to be such a happy day."

The housekeeper entered the breakfast nook, bringing a plate of scrambled eggs, blackberry muffins, and cheese grits for Mona. Chloe received diced country ham. Both ate happily while Farley continued reading his newspaper.

"Bloody hell," Farley blurted out.

"What is it?"

"Nothing about Jellybean in the newspaper again. It's so odd."

"How did you find out?"

"My maid told me."

"So, Jellybean's death is not verified. If it was, there would be a mention of it in the paper. Perhaps your maid is wrong. Maybe it was someone else who died," Mona suggested.

"Jellybean is kind of hard to misidentify."

"Jellybean might still be alive. There's hope."

Farley gave her a sour look. "Whatever gets you through the day."

"I'll hold onto any sliver of hope."

The housekeeper stuck her head in the breakfast nook. "Miss Mona, there's a call for you.

Something about Mr. Ruth finding his way to your wine cellar this morning."

"Tell them I'm on my way, and thank you for a lovely breakfast." Mona took a last sip of coffee and patted her mouth with the linen napkin. "My day begins."

Farley folded the newspaper and rose from his chair. "I'll help you get the *Sultan of Swat* into the shower and sober him up."

"I have no intention of going anywhere near Ruth in his condition. You and Thomas can deal with the *Sultan of Swat* until Kenesaw takes over."

"You know what else he's called?"

"No, and I don't care."

"The *King of Swing*. The *Big Bam*. The *Caliph of Clout*."

Laughing, Mona said, "Oh, shut up. Stick to cricket, honey of mine."

"You do realize you have an American icon in your house."

"Yes, an American hero who is drunk as a skunk at the moment."

"I have never understood that phrase. Do skunks get drunk? We say drunk as a lord. Now THEY get good and drunk."

"Which is not high praise for you lordships."

"There is something in what you say, but let's go to perform our task at hand and sober up *The Bambino*. Come on, Chloe, you mangy mutt."

"I told you not to insult my dog," Mona protested, getting up to leave.

"Oh, shut up now," Farley teased, patting Mona on the fanny.

She turned around and pulled Farley's nose.

"Hey, that hurts."

"Serves you right for slapping a lady on the tush."

"I hardly call that a slap. Don't I do anything to please you?"

Mona leaned against Farley and gave him a kiss on the cheek. "Everything you do pleases me. I just don't want to seem too easy."

Farley wrapped his arms around Mona. "I can't wait until this day is over, and the *King of Swing* along with Alice and Nithercott are gone. I want you all to myself for a very long time. I'm going to kiss you and pat your little fanny as much as I want."

"You're taking too many liberties with me, sir."

"Do you really care, Mona?"

Mona caressed Farley's face. "No, Robert, I don't."

"Then let's get Ruth sober and get this day over with."

"I'm with you. Chloe, come." Chloe ran ahead, barking happily as Mona and Farley ran hand-in-hand over to Moon Manor, determined to get through the day.

26

The gates to Mooncrest Farm were thrown open at noon to a waiting line of vehicles, which blocked the road in both directions. Sheriff Monahan posted deputies to direct the traffic into two mowed pastures where Mooncrest farmhands awaited to signal cars where to park. All patrons were instructed to walk to a third field where the local high school's football grandstands had been rebuilt in front of a makeshift miniature baseball diamond. Booths and tables were arrayed along the pathways hocking food, drink, various cakes and pies, embroidered pillowcases, knitted baby shoes, and handmade aprons. There was even a kissing booth staffed by the Frontier Nursing Service nurses—one kiss on the cheek for a nickel or a dime for a quick peck on the lips.

A line of bachelors and teenage boys curled around the booth.

Three tents were set up at the back of the field—one for nursing mothers and those with small children, one for females over the age of twelve, and one for men of any age. Each tent had private portable privies set up as well as hand washing stations. People washed their hands by pressing the knobs on the bottom of old bourbon barrels holding spring water. To wash their hands, people let the water fall on to their hands and then onto the ground which got soggy with use.

Violet was in charge of the water and found it difficult to keep up with the demand. She finally got Samuel and two other men to help her. She drove around to the stations where the men jumped off and filled the great barrels. As they poured water into the containers, Violet dropped straw around the water stations so folks' shoes wouldn't get muddy. At one water station, she caught a young sprout deliberately holding the knob, letting the water flow out. Violet scolded, "You know you're not supposed to do that. Get going before I tell your mother."

At twelve-thirty, Mona drove up to the front gates where twelve men worked beside the sheriff and his men. Frustrated the lines were not moving fast enough, drivers honked their horns repeatedly. It made quite a racket.

"Burl, how many cars have gone through?"

"Over a thousand. We can't handle much more, Miss Mona."

"Do your best, Burl. Mr. Ruth goes on at one. That gives us a half an hour to get these cars into the fields."

"I think everyone in Lexington is coming."

Mona smiled. "Baseball is America's national pastime. Everyone wants to see the great man."

"Should I close the gates at one, Miss?"

"Let everyone in. Have them park alongside the driveway or the roadside if the fields fill up. Use some of our hay wagons to move people in and out. We'll do our best to accommodate everyone."

"All right, but it's gonna ruin the lawn. Mr. Gallo won't like that."

"Mr. Gallo has plenty of grass seed to replant. I've got to go. Good luck." Mona drove her car back to the baseball field and waited nervously at the grandstands for the nation's favorite sports hero. When last she saw Babe Ruth, he had just been plucked from a cold shower, and hot coffee was being poured down his throat by Dexter and Kenesaw. As she left his suite, she passed Thomas carrying a large breakfast tray laden with over-easy eggs, bacon, hotcakes, biscuits with gravy, sliced chilled tomatoes, orange juice, and Thomas' secret concoction for hangovers.

She looked at her watch. It was getting close to one. She gazed at the stands, studying the crowd. Everyone was in their Sunday best, but their Sunday best did not hide haggard faces beaten down by hard living. Most of the crowd were thin, living on greens, potatoes, and corn-bread. The women wore white gloves and frocks sewn from feed sacks, the men dressed in patched overalls, and many of the children were barefoot, but their humble circumstances did not hide the hope in their eyes that life would get better. These people barely scrimped by and bore the brunt of sacrificing in the country.

Mona felt ashamed to be taking twenty-five cents from them. She looked down at her nice day dress and fashionable shoes. How was she going to introduce Babe Ruth in front of all these people feeling the way she did?

Mona's Daimler pulled out onto the field. The people cheered.

Jetta ran over to Mona. "He's in the car. He's coherent. Just introduce him."

Deciding to put her best foot forward, Mona stepped out in front of the stands and held up her hand for the people to cease cheering. "My name is Mona Moon, and I and the entire Moon family wish to thank you all for coming. All the profits from today's event will be split among several organizations—mainly the League of Women Voters and the Frontier Nursing Service. I see Mary Breckinridge sitting in the grandstands. Mary, will you please stand."

Mary Breckinridge stood and waved to the crowd who politely clapped. Before sitting down, she threw a kiss to Mona.

"Let me also introduce Wilhemina Deatherage, president of the League of Women Voters."

Beaming, Willie stepped out onto the field and shook hands with Mona before returning to the sidelines.

"I wish to thank the employees of Mooncrest

Enterprises and all those who volunteered to make this spectacular event happen." Mona continued, "I can stand here and make a longer speech, but you didn't come to hear me. You came to see one of America's greatest treasures—Babe Ruth. Mr. Ruth, your public awaits you!"

The car door opened, and Babe Ruth stepped out wearing his Yankees uniform with the number three emblazoned on the back and carrying his favorite bat—a hickory Louisville Slugger, the grip blackened with pine tar.

The crowd jumped up and began chanting "Babe Ruth, Babe Ruth, Babe Ruth!"

Ruth waved and took his place at home plate. Thirty teenagers and adolescents with gloves, many of them homemade, ran out and took their place on the field. This would be a story they would tell their future children over and over again about the time they played baseball with Babe Ruth—the greatest hitter of all time.

A pitcher and catcher from the University of Kentucky's baseball team strode out onto the field and took their places, waving to the crowd.

Ruth faced the grandstands. "I want to thank Mona Moon and Mooncrest Enterprises for inviting me to be with y'all."

People twittered at Ruth's attempt at a southern accent with the word *y'all.*

Grinning, Ruth held up his hand. "In this time of desperation, it's important we stick together. Help each other out. That's why you're here. You're not here to see me, but help these fine folks do right by others. I know what twenty-five cents means to you."

Someone yelled out, "That's right, Slugger. It ain't cheap seeing you."

Ruth laughed, as did the crowd. He held up his hand again to silence the crowd. "I agree with President Roosevelt 'that the only thing we have to fear is fear itself', so with that in mind, I'm going to do my part. I'm pledging ten dollars for every ball I hit over that plank fence into the next pasture. Come on, boys. Let's play ball."

The crowd went wild with enthusiasm.

Ruth took a stance at the makeshift home plate.

Newspaper reporters rushed to take pictures while a local radio station broadcasted the event. Mona had even called in a Movietone newsreel crew out of Cincinnati to film the event.

In twenty minutes, Ruth had hit seven "home runs" out of twenty pitches. Kids ran to gather the balls.

Seeing Ruth was flagging, Mona stepped out and motioned for the pitcher to stop. "Everyone. Mr. Ruth will be at the stud barn in fifteen minutes to sign autographs and take pictures until three. We thank you all for coming and taking part to raise money for the League of Women Voters and the Frontier Nursing Service. Most of all, let's give a great big hand to Babe Ruth, who took the time to come to the Bluegrass to help families in need. We are indeed most grateful." Mona turned to Babe Ruth and shook his hand while newspaper reporters from Louisville, Cincinnati, Covington, Frankfort, Paducah, Nashville, and every daily in the state of Kentucky, not to mention national magazines, took pictures.

Mona leaned over and whispered, "Mr. Ruth, you are a hit, no pun intended."

Ruth wiped the sweat off his brow. "Little lady, I'm getting the shakes I need a drink so badly. I'm parched."

"Give one last wave to the crowd and then go

to the car. Thomas and Jamison are waiting with libations."

"I've worked up quite a sweat. I hope I don't offend the ladies."

Mona didn't get a chance to answer as the crowd surged toward them.

Jamison drove the car up to Ruth and motioned for him to jump in.

Ruth happily obliged as did Mona, who was dropped off at Moon Manor.

Jetta was waiting on the stone steps next to the imposing lion statues.

"Is everything set up in the barn for Mr. Ruth?"

"Willie Deatherage is there along with volunteers from the League of Women Voters plus some of our men."

"Make sure folks understand they can get an autograph, have a picture taken, and that's all. No conversation. We can't have some gabby puss take up a lot of time, and I don't want people pawing Ruth."

"We have put up signs. Mr. Deatherage is there along with Kenesaw, so we should be fine."

"What about pre-autographed pictures?"

"We have them. Don't worry."

"How did we do moneywise?"

"All the caramel apples are gone, as are all cakes, pies, and candy bars. The Coca-Colas and iced teas are gone. Violet is going around now filling up the water barrels. The nurses called dibs on the last of the burgoo. However, I did manage to save you the last hot dog. It's in the kitchen waiting for you. We underestimated the crowd."

"A hot dog sounds divine, but how much did we make, Jetta?"

Jetta smiled broadly. "Hold on to your hat, Miss Mona. Not counting tonight's ball, we made over two thousand, but the ladies are still counting."

"Oh my gosh, I can't believe it! Thomas is a genius for suggesting Babe Ruth." It took Mona a moment to take the success of the day in before she asked, "Did we have any problems? Any fights?"

"Just a couple, but our men broke them up quickly."

"Sounds like everything is under control. I'm going to get something to eat. Make sure the men patrol the grounds after three. I don't want any stragglers on the property."

"Yes, Miss."

Mona turned to go into the house but stopped. "Jetta."

"Yes?"

"You've done a great job. Much of the day's success belongs to you."

Blushing, Jetta looked down at her hands. "Thank you. You're the first person who has let me shine."

Mona thought the remark curious but didn't reply. She nodded and continued up the steps into the mansion where Samuel waited for her at the front entrance.

"Miss, Mr. Thomas wants to speak with you."

"Where is he?"

"In his room."

Alarmed, Mona asked, "Is he ill?"

"Just knock on his door."

"All right. I'll go now." Mona hurried to the back of the house where the kitchen and male living quarters were. She bypassed the kitchen only to peek in and see Obbie and Jed scrambling while Bisaillon screamed he was overworked and underpaid. In other words, a typical day in the kitchen.

She went down a cheerful hallway and knocked on Thomas' door.

"Who is it?"

"It is I, Miss Mona."

Thomas cracked open the door and peered out. "Are you alone?"

"Yes."

Thomas opened the door and pulled Mona inside his room.

"Thomas, what's this about?"

Thomas pointed at his rocking chair where a small, wizened man rocked.

"Jellybean!" Mona exclaimed.

"Shush, Miss Mona," Thomas said. "Nobody knows Jellybean Martin is here. It's gotta be kept a secret."

Mona took a chair opposite Jellybean. "Lord Farley and I thought you had been murdered."

"I fed that rumor into the black folk pipeline. I knew sooner or later it would reach the ears of white folks."

"No one was killed?"

"Nope, but that doesn't mean somebody wasn't hot on my trail. I know when someone is following old Jellybean."

"Someone was after you?"

"Yeah, buddy. They still are, but I outfoxed them. Mainly one person, but there are more in this mix."

"Did you find out anything?"

Jellybean reached into his pocket and pulled out a piece of paper. "I have an old girlfriend who cleans in the records department downtown. She let me in after hours, and I found this." He handed the paper to Mona. "Wouldn't you say this is a motive for murder?"

Mona perused the document. "Yes, Jellybean. I think you found a motive for murder."

27

Farley knocked on Mona's bedroom door with his secret knock.

Violet sheepishly opened the door. "Miss Mona is still dressing, Lord Farley."

"Tell her she can finish in the dressing room, but leave the door open. I need to talk with her before the ball."

Violet looked around to see if anyone was in the hallway before Farley pushed the door open and entered.

"Don't be so provincial, Violet."

"You're going to hurt Miss Mona's reputation with your familiarity."

"Well, aren't you precious, Violet? I see Miss Jetta is teaching you some big words. How are your studies coming along?"

Violet smiled softly. She could never be angry with Lord Farley for long. After all, he was an Englishman, and not accustomed to Southern ways. Men did not barge in on unmarried women when dressing. It simply was not done.

Hearing voices, Mona called out from her bathroom. "Violet, who's there?"

"Lord Farley. I told him to go away, but he won't."

"Send him in."

Sauntering toward Mona's bathroom, Farley said, "Close your mouth, Violet. It's unbecoming."

Mona, clad in a robe, met Farley in the dressing room between the bedroom and the bathroom. She threw open a closet and took out some dresses. "I know I'm late. The florist didn't get here with the flower arrangements until six, and Bisaillon had a meltdown setting up Alice and Nithercott's reception cake. The top layer fell off. Luckily it didn't break. Alice broke into tears until Nithercott picked it up and put it back on the cake. We just won't serve the top two layers of cake, saying we are saving them for the bride and groom's first anniversary."

"Why didn't you leave it off?"

"Because of the design on the front of the cake. It wouldn't have made sense without the top layer."

"I won't tell anyone." Farley looked at his watch. "You'd better hurry. Your guests are arriving."

Mona pulled out several dresses. "Which one shall I wear? This one?" She pulled out a bronze satin dress and looked at it. "Ah, it's too low cut. This is a charity ball, after all."

Farley picked up the bronze dress and looked at it. "Save it for me. I like you in low cut dresses."

"So would every other man here tonight, but not the wives, and they control the checkbooks." She pulled out a black velvet form fitting dress with horizontal sheer rows interspaced with velvet rows on the sleeves. "This is sweet and respectable enough for the old gals."

Farley looked in the closet and pulled out a pink sheer negligee. "Wow! How about this little number? Hot cha cha."

Ignoring Farley's prattle, Mona nibbled her finger trying to make a decision. "I think I'll go with this one," she said, pointing to one of the dresses.

"Good, now hurry. You're going to be late for your own party."

"Wait, Robert. I have something of the utmost importance to tell you." While Mona slipped on her dress, she related finding Jellybean in Thomas' quarters and showed him the document he had brought.

"What do you think?" Mona asked.

"I think we better keep Jellybean under wraps until this matter is over. You be alert, Mona."

"It's unfortunate I won't be carrying a purse with me. I'll miss my little friend," Mona said, referring to her gun.

"Just whistle, baby. I won't be far."

"No drinking tonight, Robert. I need you to have a clear head."

Farley made the Scouts' three finger salute. "On my word as a gentleman."

Mona scoffed, "For what that's worth."

"I'm going down the servant's staircase. No need for everyone to know I was in your boudoir."

"Robert, how do I look?" She twirled around

in a red, V-neck, sequined dress which plunged scandalously down her back hidden by a sequined cape with a gold border and held at the throat by a ruby broach.

"Like a million bucks, baby. Like a million bucks."

Mona took one long look in the mirror and said, "Here goes. I wonder if I'll ever get used to this public display I have to do. I feel like I'm a cow trotted out at the state fair."

"Yes, but remember, you're my cow," Farley said, before ducking out the door. He didn't want another object thrown at his head.

Mona's aim was getting too good.

28

Mona and Farley were talking in the ballroom with Alice and Nithercott when Willie popped up with a delicate bird of a dark haired woman, saying, "Everyone, I want to meet my friend, Mrs. John Marsh."

"Very nice to meet you, Mrs. Marsh," Mona said. "This is Lady Alice and her husband, Ogden Nithercott. The ink is barely dry on their wedding certificate."

Alice and Nithercott smiled at each other.

"And this is Lord Farley, my next door neighbor."

Farley bowed and kissed Mrs. Marsh's hand. "Enchanté."

"Nice to meet everyone, but please call me Peggy."

Willie said, "Peggy is from Georgia, and she's a writer."

"What brings you to the Bluegrass, Peggy?" Lady Alice asked.

"My husband is from Kentucky, and he was a reporter for the Lexington newspaper. He worked on the crime beat."

"I'd thought she'd love to come to the ball, and John could see his kin. Kill two birds with one stone, so to speak," Willie added.

"We're delighted to have you, Peggy," Mona said.

Nithercott asked, "Mrs. Deatherage said you are a writer. What do you write? I dabble in poetry myself from time to time. Never had anything published though, except for my professional work. I teach linguistics."

"I'm afraid Willie makes much ado about nothing," Peggy protested.

Willie spoke up forcefully. "That's not so. Gee, Peggy, if you're not going to toot your own horn, let me. She also worked for a newspaper."

"I'm retired now," Peggy said, butting in and elbowing her friend.

"And she has written the most marvelous

book, but she won't let anyone in the publishing business read it," Willie said.

"Oh, how you go on, Willie," Peggy poo-poohed, but obviously delighted at Willie's bragging.

Lady Alice asked, "What's it about?"

"It's about a young woman surviving the Civil War and how she's torn between two men. I haven't decided which man she ends up with."

Mona asked, "What's her name?"

"Pansy O'Hara."

"How odd," Mona remarked. "I met such a young girl named O'Hara this month, and she's also struggling to survive. Some things never change."

Peggy remarked. "I've been looking at your dress, and I must say it's spectacular. I noticed it when I came in the room. It had a cape attached and now it's gone. The dress is very low in the back, isn't it?"

Mona confided, "It got too hot. I was burning up."

"The reason I bring it up is that I have an incident in my novel where Pansy wears such a daring scarlet dress to a party. I was having trouble with it, but now I think I can finish. It's a very important scene and sets the stage for the end of the book. However, I like the color green, so I might make the dress green."

"If the dress is so important to the end of your novel, Miss Peggy, perhaps you should name your character Scarlett instead of Pansy," Farley suggested.

"Hmm, Scarlett O'Hara. It does have a certain ring to it. I'll think on it, but it doesn't really matter. I have no intention of publishing my story."

Nithercott asked, "If you did publish, would you go by the name of Peggy Marsh?"

"Oh, no. Margaret Mitchell, my maiden name. I wouldn't shame my relatives by publishing under the Marsh name. Well, I see you are getting ready to cut the cake. Lady Alice, Mr. Nithercott, I wish you much happiness."

"Thank you and good luck with your novel, Peggy," Alice said.

Willie and Peggy moved on as other well wishers came up to congratulate Lady Alice and her husband.

Mona was about to supervise the cutting of

the seven-tier wedding cake when a man whom she had never seen before said in a low voice, "Mr. Klair would like to speak with you."

"Excuse me," she said.

"Mr. Klair is waiting in your library."

Overhearing the bold request, Farley sidled up to the man and grabbed his arm. "What's this about, chum?"

The burly man jerked his arm away. "Please do not cause a scene. Mr. Klair would like to meet with Miss Mona privately. He has important information for her."

"Concerning what?" Farley demanded.

"Please, Robert. People are starting to look. Don't spoil this party for Alice with a fight. Smile at the nice man."

"I'm smiling," Farley said between clenched teeth.

Nithercott came over. "Something the matter, old boy?"

"Yes. It seems some of the plumbing has backed up," Mona said.

"Well, that's out of my department. Carry on," Nithercott said, hurrying back to his bride. He related the problem to other concerned guests.

They melted away for fear they might be asked to help.

Mona whispered to the man, "I'll go."

Farley followed both of them and tried to enter the library with Mona, but the strange man stopped him. "The message is for Miss Mona's ears alone."

"I'll be all right, Robert. What harm is Mr. Klair going to do in my own house? And there's no outside door from the library. This door is the only way in or out."

"Yell, if you need help." Farley stationed himself by the door.

Mona took a deep breath, straightened her dress, and entered the library. She had no idea what to expect.

A rather ordinary looking man sat in one of the burgundy club chairs. He was balding, slightly plump, with an agreeable expression on his face. He looked like someone's avuncular uncle. "Miss Mona," he said, rising from the chair and looking her over. "You do have the Moon characteristics. One could tell you were a Moon a mile away. That white hair. It's stunning. Your aunt has similar hair, but it's not quite so striking. She has a little blonde mixed in it."

"Mr. Klair, we meet at last. Your reputation precedes you. I noticed you didn't come through the receiving line."

"I always come in through the kitchen if possible. After our meeting, I'll go out front, shake a few hands, have a drink or two, and then go home. I find these types of events tedious, but I must make an appearance every now or then so people don't think I'm dead."

"Why did you want to speak with me?"

Klair beckoned and sat back down. "Please sit, Miss Mona. I love these club chairs. So comfortable. Must be a new purchase after the fire. I never saw them when your uncle was alive."

"You knew Uncle Manfred?"

"Quite well. We were friends." He settled in the chair and felt the leather on the armrest. "Very nice." Turning his attention to Mona, he asked, "What do you know about me?"

"I know that you are one of the most powerful men in Kentucky and you have the police, firemen, and construction firms under your control. You have an office on the sixth floor of the Security Trust Building where you make deals with your cronies and also enables you to keep an eye on the comings and goings at the courthouse across the street. You are the head of a vast political machine."

"You are quite right in that I have many friends, and such, I hear many things. One of the things I hear is you suspect me or one of my men of having something to do with the death of Landis Garrett and trying to frame you for it. Now why would I do such a nasty turn to a pretty young thing as yourself?"

Klair gave a hint of a grin, which made Mona's stomach turn. It was not lost on her that Klair referred to her as a "thing."

"Mr. Klair, since we are being so honest with each other, I do suspect you because you are against progress, and I'm a New Deal woman. I'm with President Roosevelt all the way. Political bosses like you have held this country back. Making men beg for jobs and favors in return for votes has corrupted our government. Before the Civil War, Kentucky was one of the richest and most lettered states in the Union. Right now we are one of the most impoverished and undereducated in the nation. Many of the men who work for me don't even know how to write their names properly, let alone do their sums."

"And you think I'm personally responsible for this, Miss Moon?"

"Yes. Bosses like you keep the people poor and ignorant so as to profit by it."

"Hmm." Billy Klair took off his glasses and cleaned them with his pocket handkerchief. "Do you go to the races, Miss Mona?"

"Occasionally. What's that got to do with this conversation?"

"It has everything to do with this conversation. I understand you have stopped training horses to race."

"I don't want to continue a business of which I know very little. We currently board horses for stud and provide equine nursery services. Training a horse to win the Kentucky Derby is a horse of another color."

Klair smiled. "Horse racing is in the blood of every horse breeder in the Bluegrass, but unfortunately, it seems our poor local racetrack is doomed."

"You mean the one on Fifth and Race Streets?"

"Exactly. It's going to be torn down."

Mona shrugged. "No one has the money to bet on horses these days."

"True. The racing business has suffered greatly since 1929, but the Depression can't last forever."

"Mr. Klair, I'm sorry. Did you want to discuss the economy? I really don't have time. I have guests who need my attention."

Mona moved to rise from her chair, but Klair gently laid a hand on her forearm.

"As I was saying, the Kentucky Race Course is going to be torn down. A new one will have to be built if Lexington is going to remain the Thoroughbred horse capital of the world. The Kentucky Association is already looking for another location."

"I'm listening."

"The Kentucky Association is made up of prominent businessmen and neighbors. Many of its members are here tonight."

"I understand Jack Keene is interested."

"Yes, he is. Jack has put forth his farm as a suitable candidate for a new race course."

"Still, I don't see what all of this has to do with me."

"The men from the Kentucky Association want a place to race their horses. That's all. They don't care about making money beyond earning enough for purses and facility maintenance. Their new race track will have a nonprofit charter."

He paused for effect. "There's another group also vying for the opportunity for a race course, and their motive *is* profit. They are called the Pegasus Association. Your Aunt Melanie is a member. Both groups are rushing to find a suitable location for a racetrack and be accredited by the Kentucky Racing Commission."

"I see," Mona said, dumbfounded.

"Do you? It's why your Aunt Melanie has started a whispering campaign to run you out of town."

Mona grasped the gravity of Mr. Klair's words. "In order to sell Mooncrest Farm to the Pegasus Group."

Klair nodded slowly. "At least three hundred acres of it. There is everything a race course would need here. Mooncrest Farm already has many fine horse barns, pastures, and good roads throughout the farm, but most of all, it has clean water, not to mention a beautiful mansion which will serve as the clubhouse. An additional bonus is Mooncrest Farm's private race course you let trainers use. Perfect. So little investment is needed, except for a grandstand and restrooms for the crowds."

"Was Landis Garrett part of this group?"

"I don't know if he was an investor, but he did the paperwork for them."

"That's why he flooded my land?"

"Yes, of course, but he already hated you because of the dog incident. Where is the dog anyway?"

"Safe with a loving family. I'll never tell where he is."

Klair leaned back in his leather chair and clasped his hands, letting Mona digest this new information.

"Did you give the order to have my men beat up?"

"Miss Moon, you are not listening. Follow the money."

"You're saying this Pegasus Group attacked my guys and killed Landis?"

"I know for a fact they had your staff targeted, but you resisted mightily. Those Pinkertons must have cost a pretty penny. As for Landis, it's only supposition. Lot's of people had it out for him because of all his double dealings. He might have betrayed the Pegasus Group as well at some point. It was in his nature to be a . . . how shall I put it?"

"Turd in the punch bowl?"

"Not a very nice analogy since I intend to drink some of your punch tonight, but apt."

"You know who killed him."

Klair shrugged.

"Why are you telling me this?"

"Because I don't like being accused of things with which I have no association."

"I have never made any public accusations against you. I've only had private conversations with trusted friends. I certainly never discussed you with Aunt Melanie. How did you know I suspected you?"

"Sounds like there's a fox in the hen house." Klair rose. "I've said all I need to on the matter."

Mona rose as well. "What is Melanie saying behind my back?"

"She's telling everyone that you are secretly a Communist, and sleeping with one of your black staff. You're fortunate you have such powerful friends like the Chandlers and the Breckinridges. As you can see from the turnout tonight, very few people believe her."

"I'm very fortunate."

"Indeed. I would like to leave now and join my neighbors. Give Lord Farley my deepest regrets at not allowing him to join us, but he has quite a temper, doesn't he? I hope you send me an invitation to the wedding."

"What wedding?"

"Aren't you the one who complains about the lack of privacy in these great houses? Everyone knows you and Lord Farley are—again, how shall I put this—intimate friends." Klair swept by Mona and opened the door.

Klair's man stepped in front of Farley to stop him from rushing into the library until Klair was safely away.

Mona stepped out into the hall.

Klair's man bowed and simply said, "Thank you," before heading in the opposite direction of his master, no doubt to wait by Klair's car.

Farley went up to Mona. "Are you all right?"

"Klair gave me some very interesting information. I don't have time to tell you now. I've got to attend to my guests, but stay over after everyone leaves. We'll take a midnight drive on the farm."

"Can we park and neck?" Farley asked, looking hopeful.

Mona straightened Farley's white bow tie. "We're going to discuss murder, my darling."

Laughing, they both said together, "MURDER MOST FOUL!"

29

Lady Alice and Nithercott stayed three more weeks before leaving for England. As much as Mona loved them both, she was relieved to see them go. She had issues in her life which needed to be resolved, and she didn't want her greatest friends to witness the bloody battle which was to ensue.

The following Sunday, she invited the Deatherages, Aunt Melanie, Lord Farley, Jetta Dressler, Kenesaw Mountain, and Hazel Landis and her two sons to lunch. To her surprise, Hazel and the oldest son, Ben, accepted. Perhaps they wanted to bury the hatchet, no pun intended.

At one o'clock on the Sunday before Thanksgiving, all nine sat down to a lovely meal consisting of ambrosia salad, tomato aspic, baked trout, potatoes au gratin, grilled beets, and peas. After lunch, Mona guided everyone into the parlor for Dutch apple pie à la mode and coffee.

Hazel seemed nervous and fiddled with her napkin.

Ben placed his hand on her arm, comforting her. "Miss Mona, thank you for a lovely meal, but we must go. Mother needs her rest."

"I understand. Sorry you won't be present when I reveal who killed your father."

Willie quipped, "Dinner and a show. What fun."

Dexter gave her a sharp look, before turning his attention to Mona.

"What?" Hazel blurted. She looked wildly at everyone.

"I knew there had to be some underhanded reason for inviting us," Ben complained, angrily. "You asked us here under a false pretext."

"Would you have come otherwise?" Mona asked.

Jetta rose to leave. "I don't think this concerns me."

Mona said, "But it does, Jetta. Sit down, please."

Frightened, Jetta sunk into a chair by a window.

Mona surveyed her guests. "When I took over Mooncrest Enterprises, I didn't know there were plans put into motion perhaps years in advance, which I thwarted through my inheritance from Uncle Manfred. Aunt Melanie expected to be the principal heir in the event of Uncle Manfred's death."

Melanie interrupted, "We all know who killed my brother, Manfred. Mrs. Haggin and her husband, Archer. I had nothing to do with it. Don't you dare tangle me in that mess."

Ignoring Melanie's outburst, Mona said, "When I entered Moon Manor for the first time, I remember something Dexter whispered to me. He said to beware of Mrs. Haggin as she was *your* creature."

"That's exactly what I said. I remember," Dexter confirmed.

"I tell you I had nothing to do with my brother's death." Melanie burst into tears.

"Too many of my private conversations are leaking from this house. On the night of the ball, Billy Klair revealed he knew I was suspicious that he had instigated the attack on Obadiah and Jedediah plus other events like the hatchet planted on Moon property. Now how did he know that? I never discussed my suspicions with anyone outside this house."

Mona looked around the room. "Dexter, did you tell people about my feeling of Billy Klair?"

"You know I didn't."

"Willie, did you gossip about me?"

"You're insulting me."

"That leaves you, Aunt Melanie."

"How could I possibly know about your private conversation in this house? Why don't you grill your servants? You know how they gossip."

"I think after Mrs. Haggin was arrested, you lost your source of information and had to turn to another in my household."

"You are uttering complete nonsense."

Mona looked at Jetta. "How much did Melanie pay you, Jetta, to spy on me?"

Jetta shot up from her seat and pointed at Melanie. "She threatened me that if I didn't help her, she would plant some of your jewelry in my room, and I'd get fired for being a thief. I'd be ruined."

Mona replied, "I'm not sure I believe your story, but we'll take it on face value for now."

Melanie continued blubbering.

Farley leaned over and loaned Melanie his handkerchief. "Go on, Mona. She'll run out of water soon."

"Swine," Melanie huffed, dabbing her eyes.

Farley raised an eyebrow.

"The events leading to Landis Garrett's death started long before I ever came to Moon Manor. Aunt Melanie, I don't think you had anything to do with Uncle Manfred's death nor with the embezzlement, but you were working against him just the same. You were paying Mrs. Haggin for information as I said."

"Why would I pay for information? All one has to do is ask a servant for gossip. They like to tattle on their betters for free."

"It was specific information you were after. Bank account records. Who came to see him and whom he visited. His health. Deals Uncle Manfred was making. How he spent his personal income. That sort of thing."

"What's wrong with that? After he threw me out of Moon Manor, I still was concerned about his health. I kept tabs on Manfred for his own good."

"You were concerned with more than that. Late in 1932, rumors spread that the Kentucky Race Course was going to be razed, and a new racetrack was going to be built—eventually."

"Everyone knows this. It's no secret."

"What is a secret is that you joined a group of prominent horsemen who call themselves the Pegasus Association and want to build a racetrack for profit."

"One of the reasons the old racetrack is being torn down is because no one goes to the races anymore," Melanie protested.

"So you don't deny you are a member of the Pegasus Association?"

"Of course, I deny it."

Mona opened a drawer in a side table next to her. She pulled out a document typed with the Pegasus letterhead and handed it to Melanie. "Then why is your name on the Pegasus membership list?"

"Where did you get this?"

"It was liberated from the back of Kenesaw Mountain's Crosley radio during the course of our lunch."

"You searched my home?" Kenesaw asked, startled.

"You mean the house on my property where you happen to live on my dime, Kenesaw."

"You had no right."

"I have every right, but you need to be quiet. I'll come around to you later."

Jetta groaned and starting biting her fingernails. She shot a frightened look at Kenesaw.

"Melanie, do you also deny you were working with the Pegasus Association to buy part of Mooncrest Farm, specifically the land surrounding Moon Manor for a new racetrack?"

Melanie sniffed and dabbed her eyes. "If you must know, then yes, but not buy—lease. It's a win-win deal. The Moon family owns the property and the Pegasus Association pays us a big fat fee every year for use of the property. I was going to broach the subject with Manfred but he died before all the kinks were worked out."

"But the kinks were worked out?"

"All except for you. Manfred's death complicated things. It was a shock to discover you inherited everything instead of me. My own brother threw me under the bus and left me to the not-so-tender mercies of an outsider and worst of all—a Yankee do-gooder with illusions of being another Jane Addams."

"You had to get me out of the way somehow, so you began a campaign of assassination by whispering, but all so sweetly. Was it something like this? 'Mona tries her best, but I'm afraid the business is too complicated for her. She's going to run Mooncrest Enterprises into the ground.' 'Oh, did I tell you Mona seems awfully chummy with her staff—wink, wink.'"

Melanie wilted under Mona's frozen stare.

"When Moon Enterprises' profits soared under my leadership, you tried a different tactic. You talked the Pegasus Association into sending goons to attack my employees and stir up trouble with other horse farmers' workers."

Dexter pitched in. "All in the hopes this would eventually reach Mooncrest Enterprises Executive Board, and they would feel compelled to boot Mona out."

Mona said, "But I hold the majority stock in Mooncrest."

Dexter said, "Not exactly. If Melanie can convince the rest of the board to move against you, it would give them fifty-one percent of the voting stock."

"Let me finish, Dexter. When Melanie's gossip scheme backfired, she tried another tactic. She began working with Landis Garrett, who was a silent member of Pegasus. Landis was only too happy to oblige Melanie as he hated me for interfering with his dog, so he began flooding my land by damming the stream for starters. The plan was to cause all sorts of trouble for me until I couldn't take it anymore and resign as president of Mooncrest Enterprises and leave Moon Manor for good."

"I'm right here. Talk directly to me, Mona."

"Okay, Melanie. But Landis couldn't help being Landis. He found out about the agreement I made you sign, stipulating that if you were found to be working against me in any capacity, I had the right to cut off your annual stipend. So, he started blackmailing you."

Melanie straightened in her chair. "All I will say is I had nothing to do with the death of Landis Garrett, but I was glad when he died. Joyful might be the word."

Hazel made a moaning sound.

Throwing Hazel a disgusted sneer, Melanie said, "Hazel, quit sniveling. You wanted Landis dead as much as anyone. He was the most miserable of men."

Ben said sharply, "Don't speak about my father in such a tone."

Melanie laughed. "As if you weren't thrilled when you were told he was dead. If anybody wanted Landis stretched out on a slab, it was you. You had quite the hissy fit when you found out Daddy was playing around with a sixteen-year-old girl and got her in the family way. What made it worse was she wasn't going to stay quiet about it, and Landis didn't care if she squealed. Was Landis in love with the girl, Ben? Was he going to leave your mother for some poor white trash strumpet? What hypocrites you Garretts are, but then I would say most of the men in this room are screwing women who are not their wives. Right, Mona?"

"You're quite the lady, Melanie," Dexter sneered.

"Does she mean you as well, Dexter?" Willie asked. Suddenly this little game of Mona's wasn't so entertaining after all.

"Where were you at the time of your father's death?" Mona demanded of Ben.

Ben averted his eyes and tugged at a button on his double-breasted navy blazer. "I don't have to answer."

"He was with me," Hazel announced.

"No, he wasn't," Willie countered. "At least, not around the time Landis died. You and I were having lunch. I have it written down on my calendar."

Hazel looked down at her clasped hands. "Oh."

"Mother, you don't have to cover for me. I didn't kill Father."

"But you did cut off your father's head and plant the hatchet later on my property," Mona shot back at Ben. "You're the one who tipped off Sheriff Monahan by posing as an employee."

Both Dexter and Ben jumped up. "What?"

Farley ordered, "Sit down. Both of you."

"You knew about the plans to take over Mooncrest Farm, but what you really wanted was to cause the Moon name such notoriety, the Mooncrest Farm would not be considered by the racing commission. You wanted your farm to be the sight of the new racetrack."

"Did you kill your father, son?" Hazel asked.

"Mother, I promise. I didn't kill him."

"How did Landis die?" Farley wondered out loud.

Mona walked over to Kenesaw and stood squarely in front of his chair. "Kenesaw, would you like to answer the question?"

"Why me?"

"Because you killed him."

"What motive would I have?"

Mona returned to the side table and withdrew a certificate from the file and handed it to him.

"What is it?" Melanie asked.

"I see from Hazel and Ben's faces they know what it is," Mona said, watching their faces.

"How did you get this? No one knew," Kenesaw said, clutching the document.

"I hired someone with vast knowledge of the Bluegrass and its people. He knew the open secret that Landis had been a womanizer since his teen years. Obviously there must be children from these affairs. His family was acquainted with your family and knew there was no father for you in the picture, so he did a little digging and came across your birth certificate. It states *Father Unknown*. However, a letter was found in the back of your radio from your mother asking Landis for financial help in 1915 when you were about ten. It was returned *To Sender* unopened." Mona handed the letter to Dexter, who quickly read it.

Hazel dropped her coffee cup, which shattered on the floor. "I knew this day would come, and the Lord would demand payment."

"Give back the letter. That's my personal property," Kenesaw said, tears welling in his eyes. "You have no right."

"It must have made you furious to read a letter from your mother begging for help, and Landis ignoring her like she was a piece of garbage," Mona said.

"I found the letter after she had died. It made me sick. Landis was living like a king, and women, like my mother, were working their fingers to the bone, raising his bastard kids.

"I was determined to make him pay, which is why I got a job here. One day I was chopping down tree suckers in the back pasture when I saw him sneaking from Melanie Moon's house, taking the path by the river. No one was about. I thought it the perfect opportunity to confront him, so I did. He admitted knowing who I was since I started working as the farm manager here. Said he recognized me, since I favored my mother. I demanded my rights as part of the Garrett family. I told him I wanted what his other sons had. He laughed and said there was no way I could prove my claim, and then he did the worst thing."

Kenesaw hung his head. "He called my mother a foul name. Like the saying goes, I saw red. I punched him. I could tell he was surprised and then frightened. He tried to run, but I moved too fast. I punched him again. The next thing I knew his head was under water, and he went limp."

The room was consumed by silence.

He looked up and faced the group. "I never cut off his head, though."

"I know, Kenesaw. It was Ben like I said. He must have seen the scuffle. After you left, he picked up your hatchet and dismembered his father out of rage," Mona said. "One son committed patricide, and the other son symbolically murdered his father by cutting off his head. So much hate."

The room was heavy with silence until Mona called for the sheriff.

Monahan, who had been stationed in the kitchen and listening via the ductwork, strode into the parlor and put his hand on Kenesaw's shoulder. "You'd better come with me, son. I've been listening the entire time. Miss Mona called me this morning and told me of her plan to ferret out the murderer."

Kenesaw slowly rose. "I guess you'll be dispatching me to the hereafter in Old Sparky."

"You did it to yourself, Kenesaw," Monahan replied sadly. "Landis Garrett wasn't worth your spit, young fella'. You should have moved on."

Hazel grabbed Ben and held onto him as Kenesaw passed by.

Kenesaw paused. "Treasure your mother, Brother Ben. She's the only person in the world who will ever love you unconditionally." He looked at Jetta. "I'm sorry, Jetta. Forget about me. I'm no good."

Mona realized Kenesaw and Jetta were an item, and perhaps he had talked her into helping with his schemes. When Melanie approached Jetta about spying, did Kenesaw tell her to take the offer? How could Mona have missed their romance and connection to Melanie?

Monahan marched Kenesaw from the room.

Jetta ran to the front window to watch Kenesaw descend the steps with the sheriff. Suddenly, she cried, "No, Kenesaw! Don't run! Don't run!"

Shouts sounded from the driveway, and two shots were fired.

Farley and Dexter ran outside with Samuel and Thomas bounding on their heels.

The women and Ben sat immobile in their chairs.

Violet rushed into the parlor. "Miss Mona. I heard gunfire. What's happened?"

Mona got slowly up from her chair and went over to the liquor cabinet. "Anybody want a drink? I need one."

"Pour me one, too. A stiff one," Willie requested.

Receiving no answer from Mona, Violet turned to go outside.

"Violet! Stay here," Mona snapped.

Violet demanded, "Tell me what happened."

"I'm afraid Kenesaw Mountain has been shot.

It's not something you need to see. Would you be so kind as to pour Willie and me a drink? I can't seem to make my fingers work."

Jetta fell into a pile on the floor and wept into her hands. Her moans filled the room.

Holding each other's hands, Ben and Hazel fled through the kitchen entrance and hurried to their house.

Farley came back into Moon Manor and stood in the parlor doorway.

Mona looked at him expectantly.

He grimly shook his head. "He ran like a wild man trying to escape. One of the deputies shot him twice in the back."

Violet handed Mona a neat bourbon.

Mona drank it in one swallow. "Another, please, and after I drink it, have another ready."

Everyone sat in the parlor until Monahan removed Kenesaw's body. Melanie scurried home while Willie waited for Dexter. Violet helped Jetta to her room and promised to spend the night with her.

After giving a lengthy statement to the sheriff, Farley found Mona seated on a settee in the parlor. He lowered himself beside Mona and held her hand where they both fell asleep.

That's how Violet found them in the morning.

Sitting upright, asleep, and holding each other's hand.

30

Several weeks later, Farley pulled back the parlor drapes and watched Melanie Moon storm out of Moon Manor.

Behind her Dexter Deatherage followed, holding a briefcase, looking very smug.

Melanie turned and yelled at Dexter, using words a sailor would blush to utter. She got into her yellow LaSalle, slammed the car door, and screeched down the driveway.

Dexter grinned and whistled a happy tune on the way to his car.

A moment later, Mona entered the parlor.

"How did it go?" Farley asked.

"Dexter threatened Melanie with legal action unless she complied with our demands."

"From her demeanor upon leaving, I take it she did."

"Dexter allowed her to keep her annual stipend, but Melanie had to sign over her stocks in Mooncrest Enterprises to me and resign from the board. Dexter has sent a memo to Mooncrest management that no one is to follow any orders originating from Melanie, and tomorrow he will send out a press release that she has stepped down from the board due to health concerns."

"You now have the majority of stocks. You rule the roost."

"Nothing like pressure, huh?"

"You are going to be a very important woman, Mona Moon. Embrace it. And as for Melanie, hopefully, this will end her tyranny."

"Don't bet on it. We have boxed Melanie into a corner, and you know how animals fight when confronted. However, I'll have a few months of peace before Melanie finds her footing again and concocts some new scheme."

"We'll deal with it when it happens."

"We?"

"Yes, we. We're a team. You're not seeing anyone else, are you?" Farley asked.

"Maybe. It's really none of your concern who I see."

"I know you're not."

"You do?"

"You're sweet on me."

"Of all the gall!" Mona protested.

"I've got news for you. You're going to marry me, my lovely American cow."

"We'll see about that Lawrence Robert Emerton Dagobert Farley. We'll just see." Mona kissed Farley on the cheek and walked out onto Moon Manor's portico. "Coming?" she called. "It's a nice day for a stroll."

Hearing her voice, Chloe shot out the door and joined Mona heading toward the pastures.

Farley grinned and ran after them.

President Roosevelt (1933-1945) proposed sweeping reforms in the first 100 days of his presidency to help business and agriculture. On the day of his inauguration, thirteen million people were out of work and most financial institutions were closed by the government to stop runs on the banks.

William "Billy" Klair was the most powerful man in Kentucky for decades, even though he held no political office for years. He traded favors for votes and got his cronies elected through his vast political machine.

Mary Breckinridge started the Frontier Nursing Service in 1925. By 1959, nurse-midwives delivered over 10,000 Appalachian babies with the infant mortality rate much lower than the nation overall. Many offshoots of the FNS are still in operation.

Peggy Marsh, aka Margaret Mitchell, went on to finish her novel—*Gone With The Wind*, which won the Pulitzer Prize for Fiction in 1937. She changed her heroine's name from Pansy to Scarlett. *Gone With The Wind* is considered an American classic and is still in print today.

Babe Ruth retired from baseball in 1935 with a total of 714 home runs. He held the title for the most home runs by a baseball player in his career until 1974 when Hank Aaron hit his 715th home run, thus ending a storied record. Babe Ruth once bragged he earned more money than the president of the United States, which he did.

Lt. Governor Albert "Happy" Chandler went on to become the Commission of Baseball in 1945 and helped break the color barrier in baseball by supporting the signing of African-American Jackie Robinson to the Brooklyn Dodgers in 1947.

The Kentucky Association morphed into the Keeneland Association, and they built the Keeneland Race Course in 1936. Jack Keene got his wish, and his farm was purchased for the track. Keeneland was chartered as a non-profit racetrack, and in 1955 it gave money for free Salk vaccinations to children to help stamp out polio in the Bluegrass area. Keeneland is considered one of the most beautiful race tracks in the world.

The Pegasus Association never existed.

PLEASE LEAVE A REVIEW

You're not done yet!
Read on for a bonus chapter
from Mona's new adventure!
MURDER UNDER A SILVER MOON
Turn the page.

1

Every Thursday at four o'clock, Mona Moon held a public tea at Moon Manor, where seven people were allowed to attend. Anyone, from a lowly stable hand to scions of industry, could come provided they made a reservation first with Miss Moon's new social secretary.

Precisely at four, Samuel opened the massive front doors to Moon Manor and escorted a small knot of people into the foyer where the downstairs maid gathered their hats, coats, and gloves before whisking them away to a hidden closet.

The four guests were then greeted by a young woman named Dotty who was wearing a navy polka-dotted dress. "Hello, I'm Miss Dotty, Miss Moon's social secretary. Y'all spoke to me on the phone. Miss Moon will be a few minutes late and begs me to entertain you until she can join us. I would like to ask that you do not attempt to hug Miss Moon nor shake hands with her. Do not attempt to pass food to her." Dotty gave a quick, little smile. "I'm afraid this is not a request. It is a matter of security protocol. I'm sure you understand."

The guests quickly stole glances at each other. They had never heard of such things. Security protocols?

Dotty said, "Please follow me, lady and gentlemen."

Throwing open the double doors to the formal parlor where a fire was lit, Dotty invited the group to partake of the tea sandwiches, tarts, sliced angel food cake, éclairs, and scones along with clotted cream and jams carefully arranged on a buffet table. She poured tea from an antique silver tea service into Royal Doulton porcelain teacups and chatted amiably with the guests, answering their questions about Moon Manor and Mooncrest Farm.

Little did they know at that moment Mona was finishing her own tea upstairs in her bedroom suite with Violet, her maid. She didn't like strangers watching her eat, so Mona had her tea early and went down after her private repast. This gave her guests time to relax somewhat before meeting one of the richest women in the world.

Mona asked, "How do I look?"

Violet perused Mona's black and beige dress which highlighted Mona's platinum hair. "A bit more lipstick, Miss Mona. Your lips look a bit drab."

"Are my seams straight?" Mona asked, looking at her stockings backward into a full length mirror.

"Let me," Violet said as she bent over and pulled a seam straight on Mona's silk hose. "There, that's better."

"I'll be glad when they invent a stocking with no seams." Mona dabbed some red lipstick on and then blotted her lips with a handkerchief. Mona said grinning, "I don't want to look too much like a Jezebel."

"You look fine, Miss."

"How many are down there?"

"Four."

"That's not too bad. What do they want?"

"Pastor Harrod needs a new roof on his

church. He's here to ask if you will donate the money."

"Have I met Pastor Harrod before?"

"Yes, he supported our charity when Babe Ruth came."

"Anything off about him?"

"What do you mean?" Violet asked.

"Does he belong to the Ku Klux Klan? Longing for the days of slave labor? Beat his wife?"

Violet chortled, "Oh no, Miss Mona. He's a sincere, God-fearing man. I've never heard his name associated with anything that smacked of violence or corruption, but he is very old fashioned. He believes in the literal interpretation of the Bible and doesn't believe women should work outside the home."

Mona rolled her eyes.

Seeing Mona bristle at her last statement, Violet said, "His church does a lot for the destitute and is known for helping folks learn to read and write. Jetta based her teaching program on his." When Violet saw Mona recoil at the mention of her former social secretary, Jetta, she hastily apologized. "Sorry, Miss Mona. I didn't mean to bring up Jetta's name. I wasn't thinking."

Jetta was discovered feeding sensitive information to Melanie Moon, Mona's aunt, so Mona gave her the heave-ho. Everyone who worked at Moon Manor had felt betrayed, but Mona was especially devastated.

"I shouldn't be so sensitive. Not your fault. Who else is here asking for money?"

"None that I'm aware. There is a Mr. and Mrs. Kendrick."

"What do they want?"

"They want to introduce themselves and welcome you to Lexington."

"Hmm. Anyone else?"

"A Dr. Rupert Hunt."

"And?"

"He's an assistant professor of history at the University of Kentucky."

Mona smiled. "Finally, someone with whom I can converse." She gave one last glance in the mirror. "Let's get this over with, shall we?"

Violet opened the bedroom door and then locked it behind her before following Mona and Chloe, Mona's pet Standard Poodle, down the grand staircase. It was Mona's policy that her suite should always be locked. Only she and

Violet had a key. That way Mona knew no one could tamper with her things.

Mona had learned the hard way that being rich was also dangerous. Several attempts had been made on her life since she inherited a fortune from her late uncle—Manfred Michael Moon. Also, there had been a rash of high-profile kidnappings, including Charles Lindbergh's baby, which ended in the baby's death, so stringent protocols were put into place. Mona chafed under the new guidelines, but obeyed them. She learned long ago evil walked the earth alongside saints, and sometimes it was hard to discern the difference between the two. Better to be safe than sorry.

Chloe loped into the parlor first while Mona waited in the foyer listening. If there were oohs and ahhs upon seeing Chloe, Mona knew her guests were friendly and dog lovers. A good thing in Mona's eyes. If there were cries of dismay and frantic shooing away, Mona would be less inclined to accommodate her guests with their requests. It was one of Mona's prejudices. She disliked people who disliked animals, especially *her* dog.

Chloe was greeted enthusiastically, which made Mona smile. She took a deep breath, plastered a smile on her face, and strode into the parlor. "Hello."

The men stood immediately as Mona personally greeted each one. "Pastor Harrod, nice to see you again."

"I'm flattered that you remember me."

"How could I forget?"

Pastor Harrod blushed and his hands, dotted with brown-age spots trembled a bit.

Mona turned to the middle-aged couple with their tweed jackets and sensible shoes. They looked like the outdoorsy types. "Mr. and Mrs. Kendrick, I understand."

Mr. Kendrick extended his hand, forgetting Dotty's instructions. His wife tugged on his jacket. Embarrassed, Mr. Kendrick stuck his hand away in his pants pocket, not knowing what else to do.

Mona pretended not to notice. "So nice to meet the both of you. I don't think we've met before, have we?"

Mrs. Kendrick spoke up. "We have not, indeed. Mr. Kendrick has been under the weather this past year. We even missed Babe Ruth coming to town. I hear the event was a smashing success."

"I was sorrowful about that. I love baseball and keep up with all the statistics," Mr. Kendrick added.

"I'm sorry to hear about your poor health, Mr. Kendrick. Please sit down. Gentlemen, all of you, please sit."

The men sat and replaced their napkins upon their laps.

Dotty offered Mona a cup of tea, which she accepted before settling into a chair.

"I hope you are feeling better, Mr. Kendrick," Mona said.

"I am, Miss Moon. Thank you."

Mrs. Kendrick piped up, "Moon Manor is beautiful."

"Thank you, Mrs. Kendrick. After the fire last year, I wasn't sure if we could get the manor back to its original state, but I think our local craftsmen did a wonderful job." Mona turned to the youngest member of the group. "You are Doctor Rupert Hunt."

"Yes, Miss. Thank you for letting me come.

Oh, and please don't feel you need to address me by my honorific."

"I'm an academic myself. You should be proud of the title 'doctor.'"

"Thank you."

"I've not been able to become acquainted with everyone in the community, so this is my small way of meeting people. Dr. Hunt, I understand that you are an assistant professor of history at the University of Kentucky."

Dr. Hunt placed his teacup on the side table and scooted forward on his chair. "Yes, Miss. I am a most fortunate man to receive the post. I hope to make tenure soon."

Mona asked, "What is your field of expertise?"

"I focus on North America between 1600 to 1850, especially this area."

Mona said, "I see. I'm very interested in archaeology myself. I made my living by being a cartographer for most of my adulthood."

Dr. Hunt said, "I understand you were in Iraq."

Mona nodded. "Several times. I am fascinated by the peoples of Mesopotamia—the Sumerians and the Babylonians."

"Mesopotamia, the cradle of civilization," Dr. Hunt commented.

Pastor Harrod interjected, "Abraham was born in Ur."

"Was he really?" Mrs. Kendrick said. "I guess I need to read my Bible more often. I thought Abraham was born in Canaan."

"He was promised Canaan by God, but he was born in Ur," Pastor Harrod said.

Mischievously, Mona added, "Yes, Abraham left his father, Terah, in Ur while taking his wife Sarah, who was also his half-sister."

Mrs. Kenrick's eyes grew large. "Goodness. Is that true, Reverend? Was Sarah Abraham's half-sister?"

Pastor Harrod blushed and tugged at his tie. "It's not something we like to address except to say things were different back then. The terms sister, brother, daughter, son are given large latitude in the Bible. I guess to say that we might suspect, but we don't really know."

Mona smiled into her cup of tea.

Wishing to dispel the awkwardness of the moment, Dr. Hunt spoke up, "Pastor Harrod, are you a descendant of James Harrod?"

Pleased that someone had made the connection to his famous ancestor, Pastor Harrod said, "Yes, I'm proud to say that I am a descendant."

Mona said, "I am not up on all my Kentucky history yet, so please fill me in."

"James Harrod established the first permanent settlement in Kentucky called Harrodsburg," Dr. Hunt said, sneaking Chloe a bit of his cucumber tea sandwich.

"I thought Daniel Boone established the first permanent European settlement at Boonesborough," Mona said.

Dr. Hunt shook his head. "Boone tried earlier but failed. However, he did blaze the Wilderness Road through the Cumberland Gap into Kentucky."

"I have never understood what the Cumberland Gap is," Mr. Kendrick said.

Dr. Hunt replied, "It was basically a natural break through the mountains that the Indians used. A footpath, really. Boone made part of it wider and it was called the Wilderness Trail. It opened the door to the West through the Appalachian Mountains. Otherwise, settlers had to come down the Ohio River on flatboats in the spring when the water ran high."

"I am learning so much today," Mrs. Kendrick said, raising a cup to her lips.

Dr. Hunt continued, "I am so pleased to meet you, Pastor Harrod. I have a special interest in your ancestor."

The Pastor asked, "Why is that?"

"I understand James Harrod disappeared off the face of the earth on a hunting trip."

"It truly is a mystery as to what happened to him," Pastor Harrod lamented.

"I'm not familiar with the story," Mona said, suddenly very interested in James Harrod. She leaned forward in her chair. "I love a good mystery. What happened?"

"You explain it, Dr. Hunt," Pastor Harrod encouraged. "You probably can tell the tale better than I."

Dr. Hunt wiped his mouth with the linen napkin and folded it neatly. "Well, if you won't be bored then I shall. It's a story with lots of blood and guts."

Petting Chloe and sneaking her a biscuit, Mona said, "Please do. I like a good yarn with blood and guts."

"Really, Miss Moon," Mrs. Kendrick admonished.

"I'm just teasing, Mrs. Kendrick, but Dr. Hunt does make it sound intriguing," Mona said, keeping her face as that of a sphinx. "Go on, Dr. Hunt. I really am interested." Mona disliked someone correcting her in her own home eating her food, but tried not to show irritation. She had the teas to make friends, not to correct people's social manners.

Obviously, quite pleased with himself, Dr. Hunt said, "James Harrod was an enterprising and capable man. He served in the French and Indian War, founded Harrodsburg, owned more than 20,000 acres of land in Kentucky, and was awarded the rank of colonel in the local militia. He was respected by his community and was elected to the Virginia House of Delegates as Kentucky was part of Virginia at that time. Later on, James served as trustee for Harrodsburg. He was a master frontiersman in every sense of the word—honorable, charitable, outstanding hunting skills, remarkable rifle shot, and fearless in the face of danger."

"Sounds like my kind of man," Dotty remarked.

"Another noteworthy thing about James Harrod is that his brother, Sam, and his father's first wife were killed by the Indians. Even his wife's father, first husband, and their son were killed by them. Her father was scalped, and the son was burned at the stake. Yet, James Harrod was known for not hating Indians."

"He was a man who practiced his faith," Pastor Harrod said. "Love thy neighbor."

"Still, with all the bloodshed on the frontier over land rights, that was an unusual attitude for a white man," Mona said. "I'm impressed, but he was still stealing land from the indigenous people, was he not?"

Pastor Harrod pursed his lips together and refused to comment, even though he felt insulted. He needed a roof for his church and by God, this white haired vixen with her yellow eyes was going to get it for him.

Mrs. Kendrick asked, "What happened to James Harrod?"

Dr. Hunt petted Chloe, who whined wanting to be scratched behind her ears. "In February of 1792, James entered the Kentucky wilderness with Michael Stoner, a friend, and another man named Bridges on an apparent beaver hunting trip. James did not return with them from the trip."

"What happened?" Mona asked.

"That's it. No one knows," Dr. Hunt said. "According to James' wife, Ann, there was bad blood between Bridges and James over land several years back. She warned James not to go with him."

Mr. Kendrick asked, "Was a body ever found?"

"Yes and no," Dr. Hunt replied. "I'll get to that in a moment."

"The feud must have been forgotten if James went on a hunting trip with this fellow," Mrs. Kendrick said.

"Ann didn't think so," Pastor Harrod replied. "According to her statement, she begged James not go to with Bridges, and James must have put some credence in what Ann said because shortly before the trip, he wrote a new will giving everything to his wife and daughter and asked his friend, Stoner, to go with him."

"Ah," Mona said.

Pastor Harrod said, "Some claim that James

decided upon a 'wilderness divorce' and just walked away from his family."

"And leave all that wealth behind? Most men I know wouldn't walk away from their life's work and money regardless of how they felt about the missus," Mona said.

"I don't think so, either," Dr. Hunt concurred. "Many settlers claimed James 'worshipped' his wife. Ann publicly stated she felt Bridges murdered James out of revenge."

"What happened?" Dotty asked. She leaned forward and thought the story was better than any she read in the dime store mystery novels she bought. She thought Dr. Hunt was handsome with his auburn hair, corn blue eyes, and ruddy cheeks. He looked solid in his gray wool suit with his wide shoulders and narrow waist. Dr. Hunt had a jovial aura about him that was infectious.

Dr. Hunt gave Dotty a warm smile. "According to Stoner, the three camped on the Three Forks of the Kentucky River. We call the location Beattyville now. Stoner claimed he was making breakfast when James and Bridges went to check their traps. Suddenly, Bridges rushed back to camp where he said he heard a shot from James's area of the traps. Stoner and Bridges waited but James did not return."

Dotty said, "Doesn't sound good."

Dr. Hunt continued, "Bridges went to look for James and came back saying he saw fresh Indian tracks but no Harrod. Stoner wanted to look for James, but Bridges talked him out of it, and the two return to Harrodsburg."

"The entire story sounds fishy to me," Mona stated.

"In what way?" Pastor Harrod asked.

Mona answered, "I take it that all three men were marksmen and fearless. They would have to be to live in the wilderness, so why is Stoner hanging around the campfire while Bridges is looking for James? He should have been looking as soon as James didn't come back to camp, especially knowing about the past bad blood between Bridges and James. All three of these men were superb trackers. If James was hurt, the two other men could have easily tracked him down."

Pastor Harrod offered an explanation, "Perhaps Stoner was wary of violence from Bridges and feared the man would shoot him as well if he went to look for James."

"I think so, too," Dr. Hunt agreed. "There's another thing which points to murder—when Bridges returned, he sold some furs and silver buttons with the letter H engraved on them. The shopkeeper sent the buttons to Ann Harrod and she identified them as belonging to her husband."

Pastor Harrod interrupted, "But several witnesses said they saw James Harrod months later being held captive by Indians near Detroit."

Mona said, "If I remember my American history, families of rich abductees were usually contacted for a ransom. The Indians would have known who James Harrod was and asked for a trade in either money or a prisoner swap."

"Was a body ever found, Pastor Harrod?" Dotty asked.

"Yes, one, but it was not conclusively identified. James' friends searched for him and found some bones in a cave. The bones were wrapped in sedge grass and apparently had been dragged there. His friends claimed the skeleton was wearing James' shirt with the silver buttons missing."

"See, that proves murder," Mrs. Kendrick

said, looking about for support.

"It doesn't prove anything," Dr. Hunt said. "As far as I know, the friends didn't bring back the bones or the shirt. Do you know, Pastor Harrod?"

"I've never been able to find a record of that body. Could have been an Indian set to eternal rest there."

"So, no one knows if James' friends even found a body, let alone James Harrod's corpse."

"That's right," Pastor Harrod said, reaching for a tea sandwich Dotty offered to him. "Strange tale, indeed."

"But the story doesn't end there," Dr. Hunt alleged. "Ann Harrod claimed the three were really hunting for John Swift's silver mine, and the beaver hunting trip was a cover story."

Mona asked, "Who is John Swift? Are we discussing the writer, John Swift of Gulliver's Travels?"

"No. No." Mr. Kendrick waved his hand in dismissal. "It's an old legend. A wives' tale really. John Swift supposedly discovered a silver mine the Indians used, mined it, and then hid treasure throughout the region."

Pastor Harrod added, "Only to go blind and could never find his treasure again."

Mrs. Kendrick's hand fluttered to her throat. "Oh my, I didn't know that."

Mona laughed. "Sounds very similar to the old Dutchman's Lost Mine story."

Dr. Hunt tugged at his tie, trying to gather his courage. Out of sheer excitement, he jumped up. "That's why I wanted to meet you, Miss Moon. I think John Swift's mine does exist, and James Harrod was murdered trying to find it. There are eyewitness accounts that James Harrod was not in Central Kentucky hunting, but in the mountains looking for the mine. I am planning an expedition to the mountains to search, and I would like you to go with me."

Mona remained motionless until Dotty said, "The hour is up. Pastor Harrod, thank you for coming. We will send you a letter about your proposal for a new roof. Mr. and Mrs. Kendrick, it was a pleasure to meet you."

Mona stood as well. "Yes, it was. You must come again."

Dotty turned to Dr. Hunt, who looked longingly at Mona for an answer. "Dr. Hunt, send us a written proposal, and Miss Moon will look it over."

"I am leaving in a week. I hope you do come, Miss Moon. I'm not a cartographer, and the only one at the university is on sabbatical. I'm afraid I need you."

Dotty stretched out her arm showing the way out. "Mr. Thomas will show you the way out. Thank you again for coming."

Thomas, the butler, opened the doors of the parlor and escorted the guests to the foyer where Samuel and a maid waited with their coats, hats, and gloves. Before showing the guests to the front door, he closed the door to the parlor leaving Mona and Dotty alone.

Dotty filled another plate with some angel cake slices. "I'm starving."

"You're going to ruin your dinner," Mona commented.

Dotty looked at her watch. "Dinner's not for another three hours. I'll be starving by then."

"Quite. I think I'll have some more scones."

"Didn't you have tea in your room?"

Mona grinned, "Yeah, but who could resist these goodies. I'm developing a sweet tooth, I'm afraid."

"Who's got a sweet tooth?" Lord Farley said, striding into the room, wearing riding jodhpurs and black boots. He went over to Mona and kissed her on the cheek.

"You smell like a sweaty horse, Robert," Mona said.

"So sorry," Lord Farley replied, sniffing his shirt. "My horse is tied up out front. We both had a good romp this afternoon."

"Don't apologize. I like the smell of horses."

"So, who's got a sweet tooth?"

Dotty pointed at Mona. "Mona's got one for sure. This is her second tea of the day."

Lord Farley said, "Better be careful, girl. Don't want to get fat."

Mona's eyes flashed. "It always annoys me when men say silly quips like that, especially if they're not exactly matinee idols themselves."

"You said I was handsome."

"That's not the point, Robert. Men want women to be pretty, but do they try to make themselves attractive for women? No, they don't. They don't even think about their looks when it comes to women. The ugliest, ill-groomed man always makes a pitch to the prettiest gal in the room. He can't even conceive that he might be repulsive to her."

"I didn't mean to start a war."

Quickly placing more tarts and cream on her plate, Dotty said, "I'll think I'll take my goodies and leave."

"Oh, don't, Dotty. We fight like this on a daily basis. I always say something wrong," Farley said.

"Yes, stay, Dotty. Tell Lord Farley about our tea guests."

Lord Farley plopped lazily into a chair. "Yes, tell me how bad it was this time. I told you, Mona, not to open your doors to the great unwashed. They'll never appreciate anything you do for them and secretly resent you for your help."

"Robert, please keep your British upper class snobbism out of my parlor. What happened to noblesse oblige?"

Lord Farley held up his hand. "Before you and Dotty attack me further for being uncharitable and unfeeling, I'm not talking about class distinctions. I am referring to human nature. As long as you have something a lot of people want and don't possess, you'll be loathed for it, no matter how many good works you spend your money on."

"What am I supposed to do, Robert? Let people starve in my community when I have so much? There is a Depression going on."

"I'm saying don't expect people to like you for it, Mona."

"Money is like manure, Robert. It should be spread around a little."

Lord Farley picked an apple from an end table and chomped into it. "Who put the bite on Mona today, Dotty?"

"Pastor Harrod wants a new roof for his church."

"Ah, that pompous ass. He bores me to tears."

Mona said, "Actually, I found him quite interesting."

Lord Farley quit munching on his apple. "Really?"

Dotty interjected, "We had a lively discussion about the disappearance of James Harrod who is an ancestor of Pastor Harrod. He was joined by Dr. Rupert Hunt, who was just as knowledgeable."

Lord Farley asked, "Who is James Harrod and why do we care that he disappeared?"

Mona freshened up her tea. "He was one of the original settlers in Kentucky and is thought to have been murdered."

"Is he the pioneer that Harrodsburg is named after?" Farley asked.

"Yes," Dotty answered. "There is a legend that he went missing while searching for a lost silver mine. Dr. Hunt is going to look for it and wants Mona to join him."

Lord Farley gave a raspberry. "Lost silver mine? Where? In South America?"

"Here—in the mountains," Mona said.

"There's no silver in Kentucky."

"We did say it was lost, Robert."

Startled, Lord Farley sat up. "Don't you think with all the coal mines honeycombing Eastern Kentucky someone would have stumbled upon a silver mine by now?"

Mona smiled.

"I don't like that look on your face, Mona. You're not thinking of joining this crackpot expedition?" Farley asked. He looked between Mona and Dotty.

"A lost silver mine and a possible murder of

one of Kentucky's founding fathers—how can I resist?" Mona said, watching Lord Farley's expression as he suddenly stood up. "Where are you going?"

"Home to clean and pack my guns. You don't think I'm going to let you go into the mountains without me, do you?"

"You were not invited to join the expedition, Robert."

Lord Farley grinned, "Righty ho, but going I am, dearest, so don't get your knickers in a twist. I'll be over for dinner tonight, so tell Samuel to set an extra plate."

Mona watched Lawrence Robert Emerton Dagobert Farley stride out of the room. "Dotty, see how easy it is. If you want a man to do something, just act as though you don't. They fall for it every time."

"You want Lord Farley to join you?"

"I don't know this Rupert Hunt but I do trust Lord Farley. He's a good man to have your back." Mona rose and put her plate and teacup on the side table. "I'd better tell Violet to purchase some sturdy boots for me and get all my outdoor clothes ready. Dotty, I'm going silver mine hunting!"

2

Dexter Deatherage was apoplectic. "You can't do this, Mona. It's reckless."

Mona looked down the barrel of a revolver she was cleaning. "But I am."

"As your lawyer, I am advising you this trip places you in grave danger."

"I'm tired of parties, endless meetings, and teas with strangers. I need this trip. I need to get away from all the pomp and circumstance surrounding my life. I need an adventure or at least a vacation."

"And you think Eastern Kentucky is going to be restful?" Dexter pulled the gun out of Mona's hand. "Listen to me. The Appalachian Mountains are a dangerous place. There are few roads and what roads exist are mostly dirt. You have to go on horseback, and you'll be cut off from contact. You could run into a blood feud like the Hatfields and McCoys."

Mona grabbed her gun back. "That feud ended years ago."

"Mona, you are placing yourself in jeopardy for a kidnapping. At least, take some of the Pinkertons with you."

"Lord Farley is accompanying me."

Dexter threw up his hands. "Oh, great. Another prime target for kidnapping. Lord Farley is in line for the throne of England. Why don't you put a bullseye on his back—hey IRA—here's a British royal for the taking?"

Mona gave an irritated sigh. "I hardly think the Irish Republic Army is ensconced in Eastern Kentucky."

"Who do you think those people descended from? The Irish and Scotch-Irish."

"Robert is not British royalty."

"He's a high-ranking noble who only recently lost his royal title."

"His father did, not Robert."

"Quit splitting hairs, Mona. You know what I mean."

"No one will even know who he is. If the mountains are as isolated as you say, the people will never have heard of a Lord Farley, Marquess of Gower, future Duke of Brynelleth, ninth in line to the throne of Great Britain. He is going as Bob Farley."

"I can't help but think this is a huge mistake. What if your Aunt Melanie hears of this? She'll use it to her advantage and create chaos."

"No one knows I'm leaving. Not even my staff. I'll leave a note with Violet and be back before two shakes of a lamb's tail. You can handle things while I'm gone. As far as anyone is concerned, I'll be taking a short holiday. For all I know, this is a hoax and we'll be back in a few days."

Frustrated, Dexter continued, "Look what happened to Mary McElroy in Missouri earlier this year. She was kidnapped taking a bubble bath in her own home and held captive."

"For twenty-nine hours. I hardly call that an event."

"I'm sure it was to Miss McElroy, who dragged naked from her bubble bath by strange men. I hear she has had a nervous breakdown over this 'non-event.'"

"I didn't mean to sound flippant. I'm sure it was terrifying for her. You forget that my best friend, Lady Alice, was kidnapped only a short time ago."

"And while she was missing, how did you feel, Mona?"

Mona bowed her head. "Awful. Not in control. Beside myself with worry."

"Precisely. Remember the Charles Lindbergh baby? He was killed within the first hours of the kidnapping, and he was taken from his own bedroom—his own bed in a house full of live-in staff, and he still wasn't safe. You'll be out in the middle of nowhere—helpless."

Mona stopped cleaning her guns and looked Dexter squarely in the face. "You must stop this ranting, Dexter. It's unseemly. I know you are acting in my interest, but I can't live like this. It's not a real life being guarded like I was a prize pig at the state fair. I can't go where I please anymore. Even when I take a walk on my own estate, I have a shadow following me. It's downright creepy, not to mention intrusive. Dexter, my dear friend, what I can't get you to understand is that I would rather face danger than live a safe, dull life. I must do this for my peace of mind."

"I can't talk you out of this?"

"No, and I wish you'd quit harping on it."

"When are you leaving?"

"Soon enough."

"When are you coming back?"

"If I'm not back two weeks after I've left, then you have permission to call out the dogs."

"Great," Dexter said, angrily while putting on his hat. "Just great. You can't talk sense to a stubborn woman."

Mona watched him leave the room and heard the front door open and slam shut. She shrugged, figuring Dexter would get over it. She understood Dexter's concern and, in many ways he was correct, but Mona couldn't live her life in a vacuum. She was suffocating under all the restrictions and needed to get away where she could relax and not be on parade. This little expedition was just the ticket.

Oh, Mona doubted they would find the mythical John Swift's silver mine. It didn't matter since she was looking for something other than riches.

Mona was looking for adventure!

The Josiah Reynolds Mysteries

Josiah Reynolds is a beekeeper who loves her bees, her art collection, and a one-eyed Mastiff named Baby. She lives at the edge of a cliff on the Kentucky Palisades in a mid-century marvel called the Butterfly. She has everything—money, a great husband, lots of friends—until one day she loses it all. Now Josiah's broke, divorced, and discovers she has a knack for finding dead bodies in the land of Thoroughbreds, bourbon, and antebellum mansions where secrets die hard and the past is never past.

The Last Chance For Love Series

After her divorce, Eva Hanover leaves New York City and heads for the Florida Keys. She buys a rundown motel in the seediest part of Key Largo, intending to restore it to its mid-century glory. As Eva refurbishes the motel, the magic of love returns and guests find a second chance at life.

The Princess Maura Tales

Princess Maura must fight and destroy Dorak, the Aga of Bhuttania, in order to free her people from tyranny. She must put aside her own feelings to win a war and restore order, even if it means killing the great love of her life. Danger, romance, and adventure follow Maura as she navigates the treacherous world of Kaseri where evil wizards morph into dragons, a mysterious race of bird-people train her to be a warrior, and an ancient plant gives her magical powers to overcome her enemies.

About The Author

Abigail Keam is an award-winning and Amazon best-selling author. She is a beekeeper, loves chocolate, and lives on a cliff overlooking the Kentucky River. She writes the award-winning *Josiah Reynolds Mysteries*, *The Princess Maura Tales* (fantasy) and the *Last Chance For Love Series* (sweet romance).

Please leave a review. Tell your friends about Mona.

Join my mailing list at: www.abigailkeam.com

You can also reach me at Instagram, Facebook, Twitter, Goodreads, YouTube, and Pinterest.

Thank you again, gentle reader, for your reviews and your word of mouth, which are so important to any book. I hope to meet you again between the pages.